BLOODSHED IN
BAYSWATER

BLOODSHED IN BAYSWATER

BY
JOHN ROWLAND

Galileo Publishers, Cambridge

Galileo Publishers
16 Woodlands Road, Great Shelford, Cambridge
CB22 5LW UK
www.galileopublishing.co.uk

Distributed in the USA by SCB Distributors
15608 S. New Century Drive Gardena,
CA 90248-2129, USA

Australia: Peribo Pty Limited
58 Beaumont Road
Mount Kuring-Gai, NSW 2080
Australia

ISBN 978-1915530-301

First published 1935 by Herbert Jenkins
This new edition © 2024
All rights reserved.

Series consultant Richard Reynolds

Printed in the EU

To

MY FATHER AND MOTHER

WHO WERE ITS FIRST READERS
THIS, MY FIRST NOVEL, IS
DEDICATED

CONTENTS

CHAPTER I

A SCREAM IN THE NIGHT

M ARGERY LATIMER sat up in bed suddenly. Usually a very sound sleeper, she felt sure that something unusual must have happened to wake her so abruptly. She rubbed her eyes and listened intently. She did not know what she was waiting for, and all that she could hear was the thumping of her heart and the low rumble of a Metropolitan train as it emerged from a tunnel a hundred yards or so away from her Bayswater lodging.

But something had woken her with terrifying suddenness. What was it? And then she heard it again. There it was! A scream! High-pitched, horrible, the cry of a human creature in agony. And yet there was not a sound anywhere in the house. The scream must have come from the street. Margery forced herself to get out of bed, and, walking towards the window, she pushed up the sash and looked out.

Just opposite her window was a car, one of the low, stream-lined models: it was not moving, the engine not even "ticking over." As she gazed she saw a man emerge from it, a man in a brown raincoat, with a grey felt hat pulled over one eye at a rakish angle. There was something curiously stealthy about the man's movements. He walked slowly across the road, and as he came under the direct light of a streetlamp he hastily pulled up his coat collar, as if to hide himself from any inquisitive onlooker.

But his move was not quite speedy enough. Before his face was hidden Margery had seen enough of it to be sure that she would know the man again. There was no mistaking that striking countenance, the pleasantly-set eyes, the heavy eyebrows and slight moustache. It was a face in a million, and Margery found herself memorising it, though she could not tell why.

1

The man slowly sauntered along the road and vanished in the dimness of the middle distance, where the little cul-de-sac gave on to Queen's Road. And still Margery stayed at her window, watching the motionless car down below. She was in a fourth-floor bedroom (her job as secretary to a not-too-prosperous solicitor would not allow her anything more expensive), and so she could not see inside the car, the hood of which was up.

Then, after a few minutes had elapsed, she heard a footstep along the road. Perhaps, she thought, the man was coming back. But the sound of the approaching steps soon made her smile to herself. This was no dapper man-of-the-world. It was the heavy monotonous tread of a London policeman.

As he came within her view the tall figure of the policeman was somehow vaguely reassuring. That repeated scream had frightened her, she was bound to admit, but the blue-clad "arm of the law" there down below made her feel certain that everything was all right.

Just opposite her bedroom window the constable halted, looked at the stationary car with a meditative eye, and then went over to have a closer look at it.

He opened the door, and gazed inside. "Come along, sir, this won't do, you know," she heard him say, and then . . .

"Good God!" he muttered, "he's dead!" And, emerging from the car like some fantastic jack-in-the-box, the policeman sent the ear-splitting blasts of his whistle resounding round the quiet little street.

In less time than it took Margery to think over what was happening there were five or six policemen in the street outside, and a score or so of white faces at the windows of the house immediately opposite to her. After all, Bayswater is not Whitechapel, and a police-whistle in the middle of the night is not a usual interruption of one's slumbers.

And then, all at once, Margery's mind was made up. There was something queer happening, and it was her duty to tell what she had seen. From those muttered words of the first policeman, which had come up to her with remarkable clearness, it was sure that there was a dead man in the car below, and if he was dead now, it was probable that he had been dead when the dark-haired young man whom she had seen, had left him.

If so, what could be the explanation? Who would leave a dead companion in a car, parked at midnight in a London street? Who, save a murderer? And Margery had read "thrillers" and detective-stories as assiduously as anyone. She knew that in these cases there was often great importance in letting the police have information as soon as possible after the crime was committed. Then, and only then, could they hope to get on the trail of the criminal. Well, then, her duty was manifest. She must let the police hear what she had to tell as rapidly as might be.

She was not, indeed, wasting time, for whilst arguing this out in her mind she was hastily pulling a pair of dainty slippers on her feet, and wrapping her dressing-gown around her.

Quickly, she slipped down the stairs, and out of the front door. There she was met by a policeman who greeted her with a stony stare.

"If you don't mind, miss," he said, "will you tell me what you want? You see, there's been a crime committed here, and we don't want a lot of strangers around."

"Oh, that's all right, constable," she said breathlessly, "I think I have some information to give. You see, my bedroom window is just above here, and I saw a man get out of that car."

"Is that so, miss?" he asked with quickened interest, "well, in that case, I think that you'd better speak to the Inspector here."

A tall, grey-haired man in plain clothes came forward. He looked at her with eyes that seemed to pierce her through and through, and then, after a considerable pause, he spoke.

"You have some information?" he asked, "well, let me have it as quickly as possible, please. This is a murder case, and there's no time to lose."

Margery felt a little faint. So it was murder, then! With an effort she pulled herself together, and smiled at him rather wanly.

"And you are . . .?" she said.

"Scotland Yard," he answered briefly, "happened to be down here on another case, and hurried round as soon as I heard the whistle. Shelley is the name, Detective-Inspector Henry Shelley. And now, will you please give me your information. As I said, it is a case in which we can't afford to lose a minute."

"Certainly, Inspector," she said, with another smile, and proceeded to tell what she had seen.

"Wait a minute," he said, when she started to give her description of the man who had left the car, "would you recognise him if you saw him again?"

"I certainly should," Margery told him, "he pulled his coat-collar up when he came to that lamp there"—she pointed—"but it was really too late. I had seen his face before that."

"You think that he was trying to prevent anyone who happened to be about from seeing his face?" asked Shelley.

"That was the impression I got, certainly," was the reply.

Shelley grunted non-commitally.

"Excuse me, Inspector," said Margery softly, "but would you satisfy my curiosity by telling me who the murdered man is?"

"Don't see why I shouldn't," Shelley answered, "it'll be in all the papers tomorrow, anyhow. He is Sir Henry Henshaw, the famous racing-motorist."

"Oh!" A little indrawn breath of excitement was all that Margery permitted herself. But the name was enough to make her realise that this was to be one of the great criminal cases of the year. Sir Henry Henshaw, famous in all the civilised world for the daring way he drove, the man who had flirted with death a thousand times, the winner of the Ulster T.T., of the Isle of Man T.T., and of countless races on the Continent and in America. And he was murdered!

She grew conscious that the detective was watching her closely, with a look of cold but cynical scrutiny in his eyes.

"Know him?" he queried at length.

"I've heard of him, of course," she admitted, "and I've even seen him racing at Brooklands a couple of times. But as for knowing him personally, no I can't say that I did."

By this time an ambulance had arrived, and the remains of Sir Henry Henshaw were being removed from the racing-car in the arms of two stalwart policemen, into the ambulance.

"Do you want me any more now, Inspector?" she asked, when these arrangements had been carried out.

"Well," he said thoughtfully, "I suppose you won't want to lose your beauty sleep, but you'll have to come along to Scotland Yard sometime, and make a statement, you know. Might as well do it now as later, if you don't mind losing an hour or two of your rest."

"Of course I'll come," she announced, "I don't suppose that I should sleep a wink in any case, after all this excitement."

"Right-ho," he said cheerily, "so if you'll just pop in and get dressed, I'll have a taxi ready by the time you come out again."

Margery dressed in record time, to the accompaniment of a quick-fire series of questions, hurled at her through the door by Jean McKean, the little Irish girl who had the room next to hers.

She answered Jean as vaguely as possible, and, within ten minutes at the most she was standing outside the front door of the house, fully dressed, awaiting whatever further excitement the night should bring.

"Oh, here you are, Miss Latimer," said the Inspector, apparently coming from nowhere, "quite ready? Good! So we'll just get that statement of yours down in writing before you forget it."

"I don't think I shall ever forget it, Inspector," she said, getting into the waiting taxi, "that horrible scream!"

"Yes," he said gravely, "a man has a way of screaming when he sees death staring him in the face, you know—and an unpleasant form of death at that."

"Then," she found herself stammering, "then, you really think . . .?"

"I really think that you came within an ace of seeing a murder committed," he said, "and I know that in consequence you are going to be a very valuable witness for the prosecution—when we lay our hands on the gentleman whom you saw getting out of that car."

"He was the murderer, then?" asked Margery.

"Not a doubt of it, to my mind," said Shelley, "for Henshaw was stabbed in the back with as nasty-looking a knife as I remember coming across. And a man who stabs doesn't vanish into thin air, you know. There were two stabs, which doubtless accounts for the two screams that you heard."

Margery gasped again. Quite possibly these affairs of sudden death came all in the day's work at Scotland Yard, but to a secretary, even though she might be secretary to a solicitor with one of the most extensive criminal practices in the country, it was all terribly exciting.

"And now, about yourself, Miss Latimer," said Shelley, "can you tell me a little about who you are and what you do? I like to know something about my witnesses, you know. A lot of red tape, really, but at the Yard they like us to trace out the antecedents of everyone connected with a case, even though they may be only witnesses."

So Margery found herself telling this kindly middle-aged man all about herself. She explained how she had been orphaned at an early age, and how Mr. Bellingham, the solicitor of Chancery Lane, had acted as her guardian until three years earlier, at which date he had offered her a post in his office.

"Bellingham, eh?" said Shelley, with a nod and a smile, "so you're his secretary. Very interesting, very interesting." And he nodded again, as if he were pigeonholing this information for future use.

"And how do you like the job?" he asked, after a momentary pause.

"I like it very well," she said, "very well, indeed. I deal mainly with the civil side of his work, of course. Mr. Jenkins, his other secretary, has most to do with the criminal practice."

Whilst this conversation was going on they had moved rapidly along the familiar streets of Bayswater and Paddington, and now they were driving down to Trafalgar Square, *en route* for Whitehall and Scotland Yard.

Soon they arrived outside the impressive buildings, at which Margery had often gazed with bated breath, and Shelley paid off the taxi-driver, and led the way into the famous home of Britain's most efficient police force.

"I'll guarantee that you've never been here before, Miss Latimer," he said with a pleasant smile, "cigarette?" And he held out his case to her.

"Thank you, Inspector," she said, smiling also, "and now what do I do?"

"You repeat, in the presence of a shorthand expert, what you told me an hour or so ago," he said, "your statement will be typed out in a few minutes, and you will sign it. That's really all that we want with you for the moment. Not so very terrible, after all, is it?" Shelley had seen that the sensitive girl, after all the cumulative excitements of the evening, had been nervous with the prospect of a long and tiresome interview ahead of her.

She looked at him gratefully. "So that is all?" she asked, "not as bad as I had thought. No third degree or anything like that, Inspector?"

"Nothing like that," he said. "I'm very much afraid that you've been reading the more sensational portions of our national press, Miss Latimer. No, you can rest assured that the only people we deal with like that are the criminals that we know to be guilty. And they don't deserve anything but ruthless treatment, you know."

Margery could not restrain a smile at the shorthand expert. Somehow she had expected a girl, something like the shorthand-typists among whom the bigger part of her working life was spent. And this stolid-looking policeman was strikingly different from them.

"Now, then, Miss Latimer, please," said Shelley.

Her statement did not take long to repeat, Shelley interpolating tactful questions when she showed signs of wandering from the point, and then it seemed only a minute or two before a neatly-typed copy of her statement was before her, ready for her signature.

"Do you know," asked Shelley, when this rite was performed, "that it is nearly two o'clock? I'm afraid that the good Mr. Bellingham will have to wait a little for his charming secretary in the morning, won't he?" And he made an ironical little bow, rising from his seat as he did so. His meaning was clear: her part of the night's work was over.

"Oh, I shall be there at half-past nine as usual," she said, "but what about yourself, Inspector?"

Again he smiled that cynical smile of his.

"One of the well-known qualifications of the successful detective, my dear young lady," he replied, "is the ability to do without sleep when necessary."

Margery was shepherded out of the room by the stolid shorthand expert, and led, with equal skill, down the stairs, and into the waiting taxi.

The time sped by with unbelievable speed, and, within a minute or so, it seemed to Margery, she was back in her little bedroom.

A timid tap came at the door. It was Jean McKean.

"Wherever have ye been, Margery, dear?" she asked, "we've been worrying ourselves to death about ye."

"Scotland Yard," said Margery, continuing her undressing, and not bothering to unlock the door.

"Scotland Yard? The dear knows where ye'll be going to next," said Jean, "and whatever did they want with ye there?"

"That's a secret, Jean, for the moment," Margery told her, "but now you must go to sleep and so must I. We shall read all about it in the papers in the morning."

With that Jean had, perforce, to be content. Margery was resolved to tell her friend nothing more. After all, even if she were involved in an exciting murder case, she was still Victor Bellingham's secretary, and she had still to go to work in the morning.

In less than seven hours she had to be at her desk in Chancery Lane, and the best part of those seven hours must be spent in slumber. It was true that this was her resolve, but it is to be feared that her slumbers were not undisturbed. She found herself dreaming of all sorts of wild things, from murders to taxi accidents, and it was a very weary Margery Latimer who forced herself to get out of bed and dress again at eight o'clock.

CHAPTER II

THE MOTOR MANIAC

A S Margery walked down Chancery Lane from the Underground station that morning she felt tired and worn, more like a girl at the end of a day's work than one at the beginning of it, but she forced herself to smile cheerily at Mr. Bellingham as she went into his private office for her instructions.

Mr. Bellingham seemed strangely distraught, too. He looked up at her without his usual smile, and spoke sharply at her.

"Get these letters done as quickly as you can, Miss Latimer," he said. He always called her Miss Latimer in the office, although in private life they were on more intimate terms. She had been "Margery" to him ever since her tenth birthday, when she was left orphaned in a war-stricken world.

"Very good, Mr. Bellingham," she said coldly, and went into the outer office again.

"Old Bell's a bit nasty this morning, isn't he?" said the office-boy, "on the razzle last night, I expect." And Margery was so little like her usual self that she was unable to administer the reproof which the remark demanded.

The letters did not take long. They were the usual routine work of a solicitor with a large practice, and did not demand any great part of Margery's attention. As she tapped away at the keys of her typewriter she found herself going over in her mind, the events of the previous night.

The morning papers had added nothing to her knowledge. They merely contained a paragraph in the "Stop Press" column to the effect that Sir Henry Henshaw, the famous racing motorist, had been found dead in his car in Bayswater during the night. It was too late for any details to be published. She would have to wait for the early editions of the evening papers for that. And, in the meantime, she knew more about the Whole business than anyone else outside Scotland Yard.

The bell on her desk rang urgently. She got up from her chair obediently, and went into the office of Mr. Bellingham, wondering meanwhile what could be the meaning of this call. It was not often that he disturbed her while she was on some task which he had set, and he must have known that this batch of letters would occupy her a full half-hour at least.

"Come in," said Mr. Bellingham, in answer to her knock, and she walked in boldly, her writing-pad and pencil ostentatiously showing.

"Sit down," he said briefly when she looked at him, and she obeyed, still wondering what could be the meaning of this. It must have been something very urgent for Mr. Bellingham to take her suddenly off her routine work and request her presence in his office.

"I expect," he began, when she had seated herself, "that you wonder, Miss Latimer, why I have sent for you now." She nodded. No other reply seemed necessary.

"Well," he went on, "the fact of the matter is, that I have been thinking this business over for some time, and meaning to speak to you about it for some days at least. But the time didn't seem ripe, somehow, and so I kept on putting it off and putting it off."

"What is it that you wish to tell me, Mr. Bellingham?" she asked, "remember that I have a number of letters to deal with, and I have only done half of them. And then you have an appointment here with Mr. Ponsford, of the British Mercantile Corporation about that insurance business in half an hour. I expect that you'll want me for that, and the letters should be dealt with first."

"Don't fuss, girl, don't fuss," he said testily, "what I want to talk about is more important than Ponsford's business, ay, or the letters, either. Let them wait."

Margery looked at him in surprise. Why was he so irritable this morning? There seemed no reason for this display of temper, simply because she had reminded him of an important appointment which seemed to have escaped his memory.

"Now," he said, "that we have settled that little affair, there are a few questions which I want to ask you. Have you ever thought, my dear, that I am getting to be an old man?"

"Mr. Bellingham!" she expostulated, "you have years of good work ahead of you, I hope."

"No," he said firmly, "I don't really think that I have many years to live. But that apart, I have decided that the time has come for me to retire from my profession, and go to live in the country. You know, London grows very tiresome and nerve-racking these days for a man who is in sight of seventy."

Margery could scarcely believe her ears. That serene old man, with his iron-grey hair and military-looking moustache, had been the same ever since she had known him, which was for some fifteen years. It seemed impossible that the strain of modern London could be so telling on him.

"Yes," he said, smiling with something like his old vivacity, am going to retire, and so it is time, Margery, my dear, for you to be looking for another job."

"I can't believe it!" Margery gasped, "life seems to be just one surprise after another."

"Why, what was the other surprise?" he asked.

"Oh, of course, I hadn't told you," said Margery. "You know, last night I went to Scotland Yard. I am an important witness in the case of the murder of Sir Henry Henshaw."

And then she gazed at Mr. Bellingham in amazement. For one moment he looked at her, his teeth bared in a snarl which seemed almost bitterly antagonistic, and then, without another word, he dropped across his desk in a dead faint!

Margery hurriedly summoned two of the clerks, and, between them, they managed to get the old man's limp body into a comfortable armchair.

A glass of brandy, forced between his pale lips, soon brought him back to consciousness, and he looked around him apologetically.

"I'm sorry," he muttered, "very sorry. But my heart . . . not what it used to be, you know."

With a peremptory gesture, he drove the two clerks from the room, and then turned to Margery with a pitiful smile.

"Forgive me," he said, "but I have these sudden spasms nowadays. Have had them for some time, as a matter of fact, but I didn't want you to know anything about it, my dear. That is one of the reasons why I am retiring in a month or two. I shall take a quiet little place in the country, and potter about with roses and carnations, do a bit of fishing and a bit of shooting, perhaps. As a matter of fact, I've got my eye on a place in Surrey now."

"Are you sure that you're all right?" asked Margery.

"Right as rain," he said cheerfully, "right as rain, my dear, until the next time. And that won't be for some days, at any rate."

But somehow, in spite of the unwonted use of her Christian name, and the repeated terms of endearment which he used, Margery got the impression that her employer had some strange lurking fear at the back of his mind. There was something which he was keeping from her, something which he had no suspicion that she knew.

"And now," he went on, after a moment, "about this job of yours. I have, as I said, been contemplating my retirement from London for some time, and I've kept my eyes—and my ears—open about the possibility of some sort of job for you. And I've got hold of something which will, I think, provide you with what you want."

"How do you know what I want, Mr. Bellingham?" she asked.

"Perhaps I should rather have said what I think you want, or what I should like you to want," he said, "but in any case the words don't matter. The main thing is the job. And this is it." He fumbled at some papers on his desk.

"Have you ever heard," he asked, "of the National Anti-Speed Association?"

"I can't say that I have," Margery admitted.

"Well," he said, "as far as I can make out, it's run by a young man who, unlike the average young man of today, has a great dislike of speed in all its shapes and forms. Racing motor-cars, aeroplanes, speedboats, all these things he wants to do away with. And he's got a good deal of money, derived from ground rents in one of these rapidly-expanding suburbs, so I understand, and has started this association to do away with all these things."

"Sounds pretty ambitious and pretty hopeless," said Margery.

"That's what I told him," said her employer, "but that's neither here nor there. The fact is, he wants a secretary for his association, and he is prepared to pay well for the right lady. My idea is that you should be the lady."

"But there's nothing that I like more than a ride in a good speedy car," objected Margery, "and the only time that I went up in an aeroplane I enjoyed it no end."

"That doesn't matter. The fellow's scheme is a crack-brained impossibility, anyhow," said the old man, "and the salary offered is—five hundred pounds a year!"

"Who is this secretary's dream-employer?" asked Margery sarcastically.

"His name is John Cook," said Mr. Bellingham, "he lives at Hampstead, and he has an office in one of the courts off Fleet Street—Crane Court, I think it is."

"Do I go along there and interview the gentleman?"

"No," said Mr. Bellingham, "he's coming here this morning, in about ten minutes or so. I've done a little business with him, in connection with these ground rents of his, and I told him about you. I thought that he might be inclined to take you on for the job, and he said that he would like to talk it over with you."

"Well," said Margery, "it sounds as if it might be interesting." And with that she left him.

When she was in the outer office the telephone-bell sounded.

"Is Miss Margery Latimer there, please?" asked the voice at the other end.

"Speaking," she said briefly.

"This is Shelley, Miss Latimer," said the voice, "I won't say anything more. Telephones have ears, you know. There is such a thing as tapping them, you know."

"Yes," she said, understanding that the Inspector did not wish his position to be announced to all and sundry, "I understand, Mr. Shelley. What is it that you want?"

"Just a little friendly warning," he said, "if you have anything to do which leads you into unfamiliar streets, let me know first, and I will see that you are protected. Also, were you thinking of changing your employment?"

"I wasn't, but my employer was," she answered, "why?"

"Don't definitely accept any new job," he said, "until you've let me know all about it, and given me time to make enquiries about the prospective employer. You have valuable information in your possession, you know, and I think that our friends of last night might try to get hold of you and ensure your silence. That's all. Good-bye." The line went dead, and Margery replaced the receiver thoughtfully.

What could it mean? Was she in any personal danger? That had not occurred to her before, but she saw now that she was, as far as she knew, the only person who had seen that dark young man leave the car on the previous night. And when there was only one really dangerous witness in a murder charge, there was always the danger that that witness might disappear. She shivered. What silly ideas was she getting into her head? After all, hadn't she a detective-inspector of Scotland Yard behind her? He, at any rate, would protect her against whatever evils might be in her way.

Again Mr. Bellingham's private bell went, and she arose, once more gathered up her writing-pad and pencil, and made for his private office.

She heard voices as she went towards the door. Clearly he had someone with him, someone who had entered by the other door from the corridor, which did not necessitate going through the outer office. Then she remembered, simultaneously, what Mr. Bellingham had said about expecting this mysterious Mr. John Cook, and what Shelley had told her about the risks of taking on a new job. Well, this National Anti-Speed Association seemed a harmless enough project, anyway.

By this time she was in the office.

"This is Mr. Cook, about whom I have been telling you, Miss Latimer," said Mr. Bellingham.

She turned round to face him. A tall young man, he was, with pleasant-looking eyes, heavy eyebrows and a slight moustache. Margery could not repress a start as he held out his hand. This was the young man who had got out of Sir Henry Henshaw's car the night before!

CHAPTER III

MARGERY TAKES ON A NEW JOB

JOHN COOK faced Margery and held out his hand. For a few moments she was hard put to it to control herself, but eventually she conquered her nausea with an effort, and took the proffered hand in her own.

"I am very pleased to meet you, Mr. Cook," she said.

"And I you," he replied, "for you are, I understand, a possible applicant for the position of my secretary."

These few words, ordinary as they were, sufficed to put Margery at her ease. If this man really were the murderer of Sir Henry Henshaw, she thought, she would never believe her own judgment of character again. The thing was impossible.

His voice was pleasant, like his face. He was open, friendly and good-hearted. That, at any rate, was the impression which she gathered. And that such a man should stab another in the back—no, the thing was impossible!

"I shall want, you know, to hear a little about the position," she said with a smile.

"Well, naturally, I can't expect you to buy a pig in a poke," was his reply.

"And what about it, then, Mr. Cook?" she asked. Mr. Bellingham was sitting quite still all this time, his eyes moving slowly from one to the other of the young people.

"My idea, in short," said Cook, "is that there is far too much emphasis on speed these days. Speed records, car races by such people as that swine Henshaw who met the death he deserved last night—you can't open a newspaper without reading about them." His eyes flashed fire as he spoke: Margery felt a wave of admiration flow over her, in spite of the fact that she thought this man a lunatic on this point.

"Yes, Mr. Cook?" she murmured.

"Well," he went on, "I have decided to start my National Anti-Speed Association to combat these things I should like to see a speed limit of twenty miles an hour made compulsory everywhere, aeroplanes forbidden, and even express trains slowed down considerably. But that is a Utopian hope for the future. In the meantime my aim is to combat the speed menace wherever it raises its head, and to show up these speed-crazy lunatics who go round at Brooklands endangering their necks and the necks of those who watch them. Advertising campaigns, letters to the editors of papers, meetings where prominent people shall make speeches showing that half the evils of our post-war civilisation are due to speed—that's the sort of thing to get on with. As you will guess, there will be plenty of work to get on with in the early months."

He paused, as if this unduly long speech had tired him, and sat back in his chair, looking at her face with an amused smile. The look of stark amazement which she was unable to hide was certainly funny to anyone who did not know its cause. Margery was thinking that this anti-speed craze was the one cause necessary to turn this fine-looking young man into a murderer. If he really thought that what he said was true, then he might quite conceivably go around murdering the most prominent speed-merchants of the day, considering that they were largely responsible for making their fellow-countrymen and women speed-conscious.

"What do you think of it, Miss Latimer?" he asked.

"Do you really believe that speed is the greatest evil of modern civilisation?" she asked.

"I do." His face was convulsed with anger as he spoke. "Speed, Miss Latimer, is the ideal of nine-tenths of this crazy population of ours. The young man who goes out on his motorbike at weekends, taking his girl on the pillion seat, the middle-aged man who drives his Morris-Cowley or his Daimler (according to his means) at a speed greater than it was built to do, the speeding lunatic at Brooklands, and the poor fools whose nerves are driven to the edge of insanity by the never-ending roar of London traffic and the breathless pace of business life—they are in their way, victims of speed mania. That's what I'm out to smash, Miss Latimer, and when I smash it I shall die happy."

Margery looked at him in surprise. Whatever else this young man might be, there could be no doubt that he was an orator. She felt more than a little admiration for him, despite the fact that she was doubtful of his sanity.

"And what am I to do in this—er—smash-and-grab campaign, Mr. Cook?" she asked sweetly.

He chuckled. "You, my dear Miss Latimer, if you accept the position, will be, so to speak, my right-hand man," he said.

"And the salary?" she asked.

"Five hundred pounds a year was the figure I had in mind," he replied, "that is, if I can find the right person. And, from what Mr. Bellingham has told me about your capabilities, together with what I have seen of you here, I am sure that you will suit me very well. We shall have the right to give notice— either side, you know—to terminate the arrangement at any time. Or a month's salary in lieu of notice on my side—not that I anticipate any such thing."

Margery thought of Shelley's warning. Should she accept? Her common sense said "No!" and she had mentally resolved to ask for time to think it over when she found herself accepting the offer with thanks. It was as if the words had been put in her mouth.

"Good!" said Cook. "And now, Mr. Bellingham," he added, turning to that gentleman, who had remained silent throughout the interview, "I wonder if you would object to my taking Miss Latimer over to my office for half an hour or so? Before she formally accepts the position I should like her to see how the land lies, you know."

"Not at all, not at all," said Bellingham, "take as much time off as you like, Miss Latimer, but try to put in an hour or two more here before you finally finish with Chancery Lane. There are various odd things which want clearing up, you know, and which would be difficult for a new secretary to undertake for me."

"Thank you, Mr. Bellingham," said Margery, "I won't be more than half an hour, if Mr. Cook thinks that he can show me everything that there is to be seen in his office in that time."

"I can," said Cook decisively, "it's not the size of Buckingham Palace, you know."

And as they strolled down Chancery Lane, and up Fleet Street he explained.

"Although I have a fair amount of money, and shall, I expect, have more, as my suburb expands and the fools of builders pay me more ground rents," he said, "I can't afford to have more than a few feet in Fleet Street. Actually, the office is in here," he added, as they turned off Fleet Street into the dim recesses of Crane Court, "and I have three rooms on the first floor."

As they mounted the dim and narrow stairs Margery began to wonder whether, after all, she would not have been wiser to ask for time, during which she could have consulted Shelley, but, somehow, she could not feel any fear with this stalwart young man near. She had almost forgotten that fearsome hour in the early morning when she had seen him stealing, like a criminal, from the car in which lay the dead body of Sir Henry Henshaw. And yet that thought was forever present at the back of her mind, preventing her from being really frank and open with him.

"Here," he said, throwing open the door "is the sanctum! And this is our staff." A diminutive youth with red hair and watery-looking blue eyes, ineffectively aided by huge horn-rimmed spectacles, came forward.

"This, Adolphus," said Cook, "is Miss Latimer, my new secretary, who will begin business here tomorrow."

"Pleased to meet you, miss," said Adolphus, holding out a grubby hand.

"His name's not really Adolphus, you know," Cook explained, "I believe it's Jim or Dick or something. But I thought that he looked exactly like Adolphus, so Adolphus he became."

Was this a murderer? Margery asked herself the question again. Could a man who gave comic names to his office boy be the man who stabbed another in the back? The question sounded like a hideous riddle, and yet on its answer it was quite possible that her whole future depended. There was something in her heart which mocked at the idea of Cook's being the murderer of Henshaw, and yet . . . and yet . . . she could not quite rid herself of the thought of what she had seen in Bayswater.

"Three rooms, as I told you, Miss Latimer," Cook was saying, Adolphus having retired discreetly into the background. "This is the outer office, in which unimportant callers are kept waiting for the requisite time to give them an idea of their unimportance. Then there is the room within, which will be yours, and finally, the holy of holies—namely, the little place where I study the "Pink 'Un" and pick out winners with a pin—or whatever I do in my leisure hours." All this was with an air of completely disarming frankness which made her feel at home. And yet there was something about him which made her feel that he was not quite genuine.

"Do you not include horse-races in your condemnation of speed, then, Mr. Cook?" she asked, and he smiled gently.

"The horse, Miss Latimer," he said, "is a beautiful animal, not a horrible monstrosity of a machine. If you want to view the downfall of modern civilisation, just compare Ascot with Brooklands."

The rooms, around which he now showed, her, were, in their way, pleasant enough. Nowhere near the centre of London can be like a country house, of course, and she had not expected anything of the kind. She had now quite recovered from the first shock of learning who the mysterious Mr. Cook really was, and was beginning to settle down with him. His peculiar sense of humour she appreciated. It chimed well with her own. And in his serious moments, such as when he declaimed against the evils of speed, she thought he was certainly an attractive young man. There would be advantages in working here, certainly. In some ways it would be more fun than being secretary to old Mr. Bellingham.

But what about Shelley? What would he say about this latest move? She would have to inform him at once.

"You will have to excuse me, for the moment, I'm afraid, Mr. Cook," she said, "I have a phone call to make, and then I shall have to hurry back to Mr. Bellingham. I should never forgive myself if I left too many things undone there. My successor must not be left with too much to do, you know."

"Quite right, Miss Latimer," he agreed with a pleasant smile, "au revoir, then. We shall meet at nine-thirty tomorrow morning."

At the junction of Fleet Street and Chancery Lane, Margery found a telephone box, and she hurried to ring up Shelley at Scotland Yard. She was fortunate enough to find him in, and she told him of her change in circumstances.

"I have taken a job with Mr. John Cook, of the National Anti-Speed Association, Mr. Shelley," she said, with a little chuckle.

"Cook, Cook," she heard Shelley muttering at the other end of the phone, and then "Have you ever seen him before?" he asked. For a moment she gasped. It had not occurred to her that she should have informed Scotland Yard of this latest fact as soon as she recognised Cook as the young man in the Henshaw case. Should she tell him of the fact now? Without any intentional movement of her lips she found herself telling Shelley that the man was a complete stranger to her. Why was her voice working like this, almost against her will? For it was the second time that day: the first was when he had offered her the post.

What, after all, was this man Cook to her? A prospective employer, that was all. But something told her that she was to find him something far more important than that in the near future.

"Will you hold on a moment, Miss Latimer?" asked Shelley, and she complied readily enough.

He had gone off to look up this National Anti-Speed Association, she supposed. At any rate, there didn't seem to be any other reason why he should leave her like this, the earpiece of the phone glued to her ear, and the traffic of one of London's busiest streets humming all around her.

But it was not for long. Soon he returned, and, with an anxious: "You there, Miss Latimer?" resumed the conversation.

"What sort of a fellow is this Cook? What does he look like, I mean?" he asked.

Margery gave his description, as well as she could, wondering all the while what this was leading up to.

"Sure you've never seen him before?" persisted the detective.

"Sure!" she said. There was no doubt in her mind now. If Scotland Yard was after Cook for some reason, then she was going to protect him as well as she could. She did not ask herself what were her motives for this action. She just acted instinctively.

"Well, I suppose you know best," said Shelley doubtfully, "but I should have thought——" He broke off.

"If I keep you posted with particulars of my movements, I suppose that will be all right, anyhow," she said.

"Have to be, I suppose," grumbled Shelley, "so good-bye for the time."

"Good-bye," she said, and strolled slowly up Chancery Lane to her old office.

As she approached the office of Mr. Bellingham, however, she saw that there was a crowd gathered around the entrance.

She pushed her way through, only to be stopped by a policeman in the doorway.

"What's the meaning of this?" she asked.

"Sorry, miss, but you can't go in. There's been a crime committed," he said.

"What do you mean, a crime?" she asked, "and in any case, you will have to let me go up. I work here."

"Oh, in that case, miss, I suppose that I must let you pass," he said, "all clear up there?" He shouted up the stairs to some unseen comrade above.

"All clear!" said a voice.

"Right, miss," said the policeman, "then you can go up. But don't look too closely at anything that happens to be about. You might get a shock."

Margery was seriously frightened by now. "It's not, not Mr. Bellingham, is it?" she asked nervously.

"No, miss, Mr. Bellingham's all right, as far as I know," said the policeman.

In a few moments Margery was in the office, her hand being shaken by a very pale and haggard-looking Mr. Bellingham.

"Wherever have you been, child?" he asked anxiously, "I've been wondering whatever had happened to you. Mr. Cook came back. Forgot his stick, he did. And he said that you had left his office ahead of him."

"So I did, but I stopped at the bottom of Chancery Lane to phone," said Margery.

"Oh, that explains it, then," said Mr. Bellingham, and mopped his brow with his handkerchief.

"But what is the crowd about for?" asked Margery, "and what was the policeman saying about a crime? It seems as if I'm living in a whirl of excitement these days."

"I'm afraid that that is only too true, my dear," said Mr. Bellingham, "because there has been a murder in this building."

"A murder?" Margery was horror-stricken. One murder, she might have said, was, in its way rather fun, but two was getting a bit too thick!

"Yes, my dear," said Mr. Bellingham, obviously trying to control his rapidly weakening nerves, "the body of a man was found stabbed on the stairs just outside this office."

"Who was he?" said Margery, "oh, quickly, tell me who he was!"

"I'm not quite sure, my dear," said Mr. Bellingham, "but I am told that the police think it was Lord Chaney."

"Lord Chaney?" Margery gasped. "And Mr. Cook returned before I did?"

"Yes, my dear, he did, but what has that to do with it?" asked Mr. Bellingham.

"Oh, nothing," said Margery wildly, "nothing at all, of course. But, tell me, Mr. Bellingham, what does Lord Chaney do?

I mean, has he any profession?"

"Yes," said Mr. Bellingham, "he is a celebrated speedboat racer!"

CHAPTER IV

SHELLEY INVESTIGATES

DETECTIVE - INSPECTOR HENRY SHELLEY was worried. There could be no doubt about that. As he hurried round to Chancery Lane, in response to an S.O.S. on the telephone from a police-sergeant, he began to wonder what would happen next. Here was the second murder of a noted speed-merchant within twenty-four hours. If some maniac were really at work, who could say when the next crime would take place?

But as he walked slowly up the stairs of Mr. Bellingham's dark office he did not show his worry: it was the same grave, kindly countenance that he showed Margery Latimer, and she thought that he was a marvellous man not to give any indication of the amount of work which he had done since the night before.

"Well, Miss Latimer," he greeted her, "you seem to have made a habit of being around when I arrive on the spot, don't you?"

Margery shivered. The thought of what must have happened in the musty stairway outside whilst she was phoning a hundred yards or so away was too much for her.

"But it is with Mr. Bellingham that I am most immediately concerned," he said, turning to her companion, "for I am told that he discovered the body. Isn't that so, sir?"

Mr. Bellingham inclined his head with a gesture of sombre assent. "That is so, Inspector," he said.

"And how did you make this remarkable discovery?" asked Shelley. Margery thought that she could perceive a sarcastic intonation in his voice, although there did not appear, on the surface, at any rate, to be any real reason for sarcasm.

"I will tell you the whole story, Mr. Shelley," said Mr. Bellingham, "it happened just after Miss Latimer left the office with Mr. John Cook of the National Anti-Speed Association half an hour or so ago."

Shelley nodded grimly. "I know all about that, Mr. Bellingham," he said.

"Oh, you do!" Mr. Bellingham seemed mildly surprised. "Well, about a quarter of an hour or so after they had gone, I was a trifle startled at Mr. Cook's return. He had forgotten his stick, and came back for it. He was only in the office for a minute or so, and shortly after he had gone, I heard——"

"How long after?" asked Shelley.

"I'm afraid that I can't tell you at all definitely," Mr. Bellingham replied, "you see, I was very busy with some papers that I was working on, in connection with an important case of mine. But I should think it would be at any rate less than five minutes."

"Very well, sir," said Shelley, "go on."

Mr. Bellingham resumed his story. "I was saying that a few minutes after Mr. Cook left the office I heard a strange noise on the staircase outside. It sounded like a groan, I thought, and I wondered if it could possibly be some poor creature in pain. After all, these stairs are steep, and I thought that someone might have felt faint after hurrying up. Anyhow, I went out there, and peered down. At first I could see nothing, but then I noticed a vague figure in the middle of the staircase. I hurried down, and almost fell over . . . the body of the unfortunate man whom I am told is Lord Chaney."

"Thank you, Mr. Bellingham," said Shelley, "that is very clear. I don't really know that there are many questions that I want to put. As a man of the law, I suppose that you know exactly how to make a statement concise and yet get in all the facts."

Mr. Bellingham smiled wanly. "Yes, I suppose that I do," he said.

"In any case, Mr. Bellingham," Shelley went on, "I can always lay my hands on you when I want you, I suppose. I mean that you are always in attendance here?"

"Usually, Inspector," said Mr. Bellingham, "and in any case you will be able to find me at my home address if I am not in this office. This is it." And he handed the Scotland Yard man a card, which was carefully stowed away in the innermost recesses of Shelley's voluminous notebook.

"And now Miss Latimer," said Shelley briskly, "what can you add to what Mr. Bellingham has told me? Are there any facts in your possession which I have not been told?"

"Nothing, I think, Inspector," said Margery firmly, "for I was, I think, telephoning to a friend at the time when the crime was committed." She saw a twinkle in the detective's eye at the mention of her phone call, but he gave little indication that he had perceived her little joke.

"Where did you phone from, Miss Latimer?" he asked. "You see, we may have to trace the call. Just red tape, you know, but headquarters likes to see everything done in its most correct manner."

Margery smiled, "I phoned from the box at the bottom of Chancery Lane, where it joins Fleet Street," she said, "and if you wish to know the name and telephone number of the friend with whom I was talking, I shall be pleased to give them to you."

"I don't know that that is really necessary, Miss Latimer," said Shelley, gravely, "because we can always trace it through the Post Office if it became really essential to our case—not that I suppose for one moment that it will, you know."

He bowed to them both, and with a polite word or two to the effect that he had more work to be done elsewhere, he left them.

"What's he getting at?" asked Mr. Bellingham testily, as soon as the door had closed behind the detective. "A deep sort of man, he is. I don't think he told us all, by a long chalk."

"Whatever do you mean?" asked Margery.

"He knows more than he lets on," said Mr. Bellingham.

"I'm afraid that I don't quite understand what you mean," Margery replied coldly. She was beginning almost to dislike this old man, towards whom she had previously always entertained only the most friendly feelings. She could not explain this feeling of aversion, but it was gaining on her so strongly that she found it difficult to speak to him without a little shiver of apprehension.

But Mr. Bellingham did not appear conscious of the change in Margery. He still treated her as he had always done, sharing with her whatever ideas he thought might be worth discussing. That was what he seemed bent on doing now.

"What I mean, my dear Margery," he said, leaning back in his chair, "is that Shelley has his ideas about this crime. He has suspicions of a certain person who shall remain nameless between us. Surely you could see that he was not at all curious about us. All that nonsense about your telephone call. I could see that he was not in earnest about it."

"Could you, really?" asked Margery, thinking that old Mr. Bellingham had more sense than she had given him credit for.

"Of course I could," he replied, "and his questions to me— why, they wouldn't have deceived a donkey. He knew that neither you nor I had any concern with this case, that we were innocent. And why? Because he had already fixed on someone else as the guilty man. And you and I know very well who that someone else is!"

"You mean . . .?" Margery was almost afraid to express the dreadful thought in words. John Cook! That was the man whom Shelley suspected. And as the thought came into her mind she felt the chilly feeling of dread stealing in her heart.

"Never you mind what I mean," said Mr. Bellingham. "You'll find out soon enough who Shelley suspects. And if I'm not very seriously mistaken someone else will find it out before he's very much older!"

Meanwhile, Shelley was proceeding down Chancery Lane, and along Fleet Street. Before leaving Scotland Yard he had possessed himself of Cook's address. He had, in fact, ascertained the whereabouts of the National Anti-Speed Association as soon as Margery had informed him of the fact that she was to start work there.

He had, therefore, no difficulty in reaching John Cook's office whilst Margery and Mr. Bellingham were discussing the whys and the wherefores of the case.

In Crane Court, Shelley paused for a moment, and looked around him. Soon he spotted the place that he was after. He mounted the stairs, and knocked gently on the massive oak door.

"Come in!" said a youthful voice, and Shelley entered.

"Can I see Mr. Cook?" he enquired of the strange looking youth whom Cook called Adolphus.

"I'll find out, sir," said Adolphus. "What name did you say?"

"I didn't say, but this card will tell Mr. Cook all that he wants to know," said Shelley, handing the boy a card inscribed, simply, "Henry Shelley."

"Mr. Cook says," Adolphus announced, after a moment's absence, "that he's very busy, and, unless your business is urgent, he's afraid that he can't see you. If you will be unable to call back tomorrow, he can spare you three minutes."

"Tell Mr. Cook," said Shelley, "that my business is very urgent. And tell him also that I'm afraid that it will take considerably more than three minutes."

This time, again after a momentary pause, whilst the boy entered the inner office and emerged again, Shelley was shown into Cook's tiny inner sanctum.

"Mr.—er—Shelley?" he queried, looking at the detective's card with ostentatious care.

"Yes," said Shelley, "and this, Mr. Cook, must be the explanation of my real business." He handed him an official card, bearing the words "Detective-Inspector Shelley, C.I.D., New Scotland Yard."

Cook blenched visibly. His teeth were tightly gripped together, and his hands held to the arms of the chair in which he was sitting.

"Yes, Inspector," he said, with an obvious effort, "and what do you want with me?"

"I'm afraid, sir, that it is rather a long story," said Shelley, "but that can't be helped. People don't usually like members of my profession, I know, even if they are innocent people who are in some way involved in a crime."

"But what crime am I involved in?" asked Cook, his eyes wide open with amazement. "I was not aware that I had anything to do with criminals. And surely the National Anti-Speed Association does not come under the heading of criminal conspiracy?" Despite the attempted flippancy, it was clear that the man was suffering from some terrific strain. The sweat stood out in beads upon his forehead.

"No, it's nothing to do with your association, Mr. Cook," said Shelley, "although, as a matter of fact, we are bound to keep in touch with everything in the way of new organisations which start in London. What I have come here to investigate is the death of Lord Chaney."

"Chaney dead?" muttered Cook, "and so soon!"

"What does that remark mean?" snapped Shelley.

"I'm afraid that I don't understand you, Inspector," returned Cook, "what remark are you referring to?"

"You said 'So soon!' Mr. Cook," said Shelley, "and I should naturally take that to mean that you were expecting to hear of Lord Chaney's death from somewhere, but at a rather later date."

"In that case," said Cook, with a smile which was meant to be casual, but which failed miserably, "I am afraid that you would be 'naturally taking' something which is in a way quite wrong. I suppose that Chaney did not die of natural causes, Inspector, or you would not be here."

"As far as we know up to the present, sir," said the detective, "Lord Chaney was murdered."

"All that my comment about its being soon was meant to imply," said Cook, choosing his words with care, and, as a result, sounding almost pedantic, "was that I happen to know that Chaney has a groggy heart. That's why he hasn't been taking part in any infernal speedboat races lately."

"Oh," was the only outward comment which Shelley made.

For a few moments they sat in complete silence, each covertly studying the other's face. And then it was Cook who broke the silence.

"Well, Inspector, I presume that you didn't come here merely to enjoy the lovely view from my window," he said, "so why not cut out the cackle and come to the hosses—or in other words, why not ask me those questions which I can see still hovering at the back of your investigatorial mind?"

"I think I will," said Shelley, "and the first of them is this: why did you ask Miss Latimer to become your new secretary?"

"That's an easy one, anyhow," returned Cook, with a smile. "Miss Latimer was the secretary of my man of the law, Mr. Bellingham, and when he told me that it was highly probable that he would be retiring, and that as a result Miss Latimer, who is, I believe, awfully good at her job, would be looking for a new post, I naturally offered her this position. Though, by the way, I can't see what the devil my new secretary has to do with the death of that old speed-maniac, Chaney."

"The connection may not be obvious to you, Mr. Cook," said Shelley, in his suavest tones, "but you can rest assured that I have a reason for every question I ask. And next, will you please give me a concise account of your movements after leaving Mr. Bellingham's office this morning? The first time you left it, I mean, not the second."

"You seem to know an infernal lot about what I've been doing today, Inspector," said Cook, flushing hotly, "and, I must say that I think it's a beastly cheek of you to come barging in here, asking nosey-parker questions like this and quizzing in my private affairs——"

"That will do, Mr. Cook," said the Scotland Yard man. "I must ask you to answer my questions, or else come along to the Yard with me, and make a statement. I should think that you would prefer to answer my questions here in the comfort of your own office."

Cook calmed down at once. His anger was only momentary, it seemed, and the Inspector's warning had been taken to heart.

"Very well," he said, "well, I left Mr. Bellingham's office, and came back here with Miss Latimer. I was just showing her around, you understand. That process must have taken about a quarter of an hour. Not more than twenty minutes, anyhow, and I should think a quarter of an hour would be nearer. Then Miss Latimer went back to Mr. Bellingham's office, and just after she had left I suddenly remembered that I had not brought my walking-stick with me, so I went back to Mr. Bellingham's office for it. I was only there for a moment, and I returned here immediately. Since then I have not moved from this chair. That do. Inspector?"

"One or two other points, sir," said Shelley. "Your statement is quite clear and straightforward, but I must get confirmation on one or two other points. First of all, did you see anyone on the stairs of Mr. Bellingham's office when you came out the second time?"

Cook thought for a moment. "No, I don't think so," he said, but then quickly corrected himself. "Yes, I did, though," he said, "chap dressed in brown. Brown overcoat, brown hat, brown tie. I remember him quite well. Expensively dressed fellow, he was, too!"

"Where was he?" pursued the detective.

"Just in the hallway, studying the board," said Cook, "you know, the board with the list of people who have offices in the building. He didn't notice me, and I can't say that I paid much attention to him. But now that you have brought the whole thing back to my mind, I remember him distinctly. If you have any doubts about the truth of what I'm telling you, Inspector, that fellow will bear me out. After all, even if he didn't notice me particularly, he must have seen me pass by."

"I'm afraid, sir," said Shelley, "that the gentleman in brown won't be able to tell us anything about your movements this morning or at any other time. He was murdered within two minutes of your leaving Mr. Bellingham's office! The man in brown was Lord Chaney!"

For a full minute Cook sat still as if stunned. "Chaney!" he said at length, "so that was Chaney, was it?"

"Yes, Mr. Cook," Shelley said quietly, "and that, really, brings me straight to my next question. You said that you had heard that Lord Chaney was suffering from some sort of heart trouble. When and where did you hear of this?"

"I'm afraid that I can't tell you when I heard of it, Inspector," said Cook, "but where—well, it was at the National Liberal Club. I am a member there, and I believe Chaney was too. But I've never set eyes on the man before today, Inspector. You yourself must admit that the whole thing came as a complete surprise to me, when you first told me about it."

"That's all very well, Mr. Cook," said Shelley, "but I think that I shall have a few more questions for you before we're much older. And the first of them will be this: what were you doing in Bayswater at midnight last night?"

Cook gazed at the detective as if he were a ghost, but Shelley vouchsafed little in the way of a reply.

"Just think it over, Mr. Cook," he said, "just think it over, and if you decide that you have something more to tell me about these crimes—for the death of Sir Henry Henshaw was connected with today's events—just come along to Scotland Yard and tell me all about it. In any case, I shall want a reply to that last question of mine sooner or later."

It was a white-faced, stricken man that the Inspector left behind him as he strode out once more into the roar and bustle of Fleet Street.

CHAPTER V

THE ANTI-SPEED ASSOCIATION

MARGERY found her new job much to her liking. In fact, the only criticism that she could offer was that she was not doing enough work to justify the truly munificent salary which John Cook paid her. A few letters were dictated to her each day, and she had a certain amount of routine work—copying out addresses, and the like, from directories—but, apart from these things, she might have been a lady of leisure.

If she wanted a morning off, Cook raised no objections, and she felt that he would not have worried had she failed to put in an appearance for a week at a time. There, however, she found that she was mistaken, for when she stayed at home for a day on one occasion, a severe bilious attack being the cause, Adolphus came around, hot-foot from Fleet Street, to know if there was anything seriously wrong. In fact, John Cook looked after her with the greatest care, but granted her every request without dispute. He seemed, however, to be becoming rather overbearing in his desire to know what she was doing in her spare time.

"Well, whither away this evening, Miss Latimer?" he would say, as she packed her papers neatly away at the end of a day. And Margery would find herself, for no particular reason, telling him how she was going to see Greta Garbo's new picture with Jean McKean, and they would discuss, pleasantly enough, the pros and cons of Greta Garbo as compared with Marlene Deitrich. It was all pleasant enough in its way, but Margery, after a few weeks of it, began to feel the restraint of this constant supervision of her leisure activities.

"Why do you ask?" she said one evening, when he had made his usual query.

"Just the interest that the model employer feels in the activities of a model employee," he said lightly, but she was not to be so put off.

"But Mr. Bellingham never used to ask me where I was going in the evenings," she said, "and I wondered why you showed so much interest in what I did."

"And I trust that I have answered it to your satisfaction, my dear Miss Latimer," he said courteously, turning away to a pile of letters which were awaiting his signature. Margery felt that she was dismissed, and walked out of the office with a curious sense of dissatisfaction gnawing at her heart. Of course, most girls would have thought themselves very lucky to have such a job. She was getting ten pounds a week for doing work which a moderately competent office boy could have performed with ease, the chief (for so she always thought of him) was not a grumpy old fogey, but a handsome and good-tempered young man, he did not metaphorically bite her head off every time he spoke to her, but on the contrary he showed every sign of being definitely attracted towards her—and he was a very rich young man! Everything, in fact, should have been perfectly lovely. . . and yet there was something which gave her cause for dissatisfaction.

It was a long time before she could make up her mind as to what exactly this was, and then she suddenly realised what lay at the root of her troubles. The office, she was sure, was being used as a "blind" for something else, and she had grown to like John Cook so much that she hated to think of any sort of deception in connection with his name.

At first she thought he was merely an enthusiast for one idea, which he was prepared to spend his life in propagating. That there were many such people about, she knew. Only one or two doors away from Mr. Bellingham's office in Chancery Lane, there had been the office of a group of political enthusiasts who had devoted their lives to fighting the landlords in this country, in a campaign for what they described as "Giving the Land to the People," and she had often thought, whilst sympathising with their aims, that they were fighting such a huge vested interest that there was no hope of success. And this National Anti-Speed Association might be such another forlorn hope. But, somehow, John Cook did not seem the sort of man to spend his whole life in such a fight. He was a vigorous man, whose whole energies could surely not be taken up with this campaign.

And yet. . . And yet. . . So her thoughts were running during the first weeks of her new job. And then she got the first indication that there was something else in this business— or, at any rate, something else which concerned the man who called himself John Cook.

She had heard the door of the outer office, where Adolphus reigned supreme, open and close again, and a murmur of voices filtered through to the office where she was sitting, immersed in the pages of a huge directory, where she was obtaining the names and addresses of the leading members of various motoring organisations.

Presently the door opened, and Adolphus entered. He looked scared and elated at the same time.

"If you please, Miss Latimer," he said, "there's a gentleman here who wants to see the boss—I mean, Mr. Cook. He says that he's Detective-Inspector Shelley, of Scotland Yard."

Margery smiled. "Better show him in to me, Adolphus," she said, "I happen to know Inspector Shelley, and I will see if it is really important business that he wants to see Mr. Cook about." And Shelley entered.

"Well, Miss Latimer," he said with a pleasant smile, "been discovering any more bodies lately?"

Margery shivered. "No, Inspector," she answered, "and I don't want to, thank you. There's nothing you want to see me about, is there?"

"No, thank you," he said, "unfortunately we haven't got anything definite about those murders, although we're on the track of the man in the car all right." Did he look significantly towards the door of the inner office where John

Cook was sitting? Margery rather thought he did, but, by a mighty effort of will, she succeeded in hiding her feeling of agitation.

"I suppose," he went on, "that you haven't, by any chance, seen that gentleman lately?"

"What gentleman?" asked Margery.

"Why, the gentleman who got out of the car that day," he said, "surely you can't have forgotten all about it already. You remember that you said that you would recognise him at once, if ever you saw him."

"Oh him!" Margery again tried hard, but did not quite succeed in looking totally unconcerned. "No, Inspector, I haven't seen him since that dreadful night."

"Ah, well," he said, "I read once that if you stood long enough at Piccadilly Circus you would see anyone whom you had once seen in London, so no doubt you will come across him again one of these days. Always running across people you know in London. And now, perhaps, you would announce me to Mr. Cook."

"What shall I say your business is, Inspector?" she asked.

"Mr. Cook will know that, all right," he said, rather grimly, "just tell him that Inspector Shelley wants a few words with him. I think that that will be enough for him, but if not, just hand him this." And he gave her a sealed envelope, addressed to "John Cook, Esq."

Without another word, Margery went into the inner office. Cook was immersed in a huge book of reference, which looked like an encyclopædia, and he did not at once look up when she entered.

"Inspector Shelley wants to speak to you, Mr. Cook," she said, without any attempt at preliminaries.

"Who?" He was clearly startled, and he spoke with a sudden sharpness which was unusual in him.

"Detective-Inspector Shelley of Scotland Yard," she said, "and he gave me this letter for you, which he said would explain his errand, if you did not guess it." And she handed him the letter.

Cook took it eagerly, and tore the flap with a hand which trembled. Rapidly he scanned it through, and then curtly ordered her to show the Inspector in.

Shelley smiled at her when she told him that he was to go in, and proceeded to walk to the inner door, without speaking.

When he was gone Margery felt a strange uneasiness which she did not know how to explain. Why did Shelley come to see John Cook? Did he really mean to imply some sort of suggestion that it was in connection with the murders which she had so nearly witnessed? It certainly seemed as if he had some such thought at the back of his mind. Margery did not attempt to analyse the reason for her long abstention from frankness with the Scotland Yard man. Why she had not told him that Cook was the mysterious man who had left Henshaw's car on the night of his murder she could not, for the life of her, tell.

She only knew, indeed, that the thought of John Cook, accused of murder, was one which gave her intense pain, and that seemed sufficient reason for not placing him in what might well turn out to be an equivocal situation. That her feelings towards Cook were rapidly changing, and were no longer those merely of an employee towards an employer who was more than usually attentive she had not yet grown to realise.

She had, however, a nasty shock, half an hour or so later, when, Shelley having departed, she was called in to Cook's office to deal with the day's correspondence.

Cook gave her a batch of papers to file, and when she returned to her own office to sort these out she found a letter which she concluded was that which Shelley had sent in. It was quite brief, and its wording made her wonder what was at the back of all this affair.

"Dear Cook," it ran, "You doubtless remember my warning a few weeks since. It was shortly after the murder of Henshaw and Lord Chaney. Well, there was a certain question which I advised you to answer. I want that answer now—and the answers to one or two other questions. S."

What did it all mean? Margery was worried, but she did not dare to let Cook see her misgivings, so she simply took in the letter to Cook, meaning to explain that it had been included in the business correspondence by mistake.

Cook was sitting at his desk, his head resting on his closed fists, and his elbows on the desk before him. In his face was the look of acute misery which she had once or twice before seen in it. For a moment he did not notice her entry.

"Oh, yes, Miss Latimer," he said at length, "what is it? Another mistake?"

"Yes, Mr. Cook," she replied, "this letter was mixed in with the others. It's a private one of your own, I think. At any rate, it shouldn't be included with the business correspondence."

He glanced at it, and smiled wanly. The attempt to be facetious did not, somehow, succeed, although he tried manfully to disguise the serious anxiety which he was feeling.

"Oh, yes," he smiled, "Shelley's *billet-doux*, I think. Quite right, Miss Latimer, that should not be in with the business correspondence. It is quite a private matter."

"Thank you, sir," she said,

"And—by the way—" he added, as she was about to retire to her own room once more, "why didn't you tell the police that you saw me getting out of Henshaw's car the night he was murdered?"

"You?" she tried, not for the first time that day, to look incredulous, "but I did not see you. I don't believe that you were there."

"Oh, yes you do, my dear," he said firmly, "and, what is more, you have some idea in your head about shielding me from the attentions of the police. Well, it's very wrong. There is never any good cause for hiding things from the police, you know. It always looks so queer when they find out what you've been doing. And they always do find out in the end, blast 'em!"

Margery was speechless. Surely he did not intend to give in like this? It was so unlike his usual attitude of complete defiance.

"But if you were there, what had you to do with Henshaw?" she asked, when the first moment of astonishment was over.

"Oh," he said, "I had quite a lot to do with Henshaw—in life. But you can rest assured, my dear, that I had nothing to do with his death. And you are a real brick to try to help me out of what looks like being a very nasty jam."

"John!" she said, "you know very well that I would do anything. . ."

"My dear Margery," he murmured, "don't I know it?" And then Margery's puzzlement was eased. She had been wondering for days why she felt so sorry for this young man, why she wanted so badly to shield him from the net which the police seemed determined to put around him, and now the puzzle was solved. It was not just the liking of a good secretary for a more than good master, it was the sort of love which she had so often read about, but never before experienced.

But she could not show this. It was not her place to thrust her personal feelings forward, the more especially as he was, as he had expressed it, in a "very nasty jam." The main thing, at the moment, was to get him out of it. Then it would be time enough for her own personal problems to be solved.

The fact that they had, almost without knowing it, dropped into the use of Christian names, was an indication of the fact that they were now in a new orientation towards each other. For the time that would have to be enough.

"How can I help you?" she asked, "anything that I can do to get you clear of this business, you know I will do willingly."

"It's no good," he said grimly, "nobody can get me out of this but myself, Margery. And when I do get out of it, there are lots of things that I want to talk over with you. In the meantime, I have to go. Perhaps you will get things cleared up here."

As he took his hat and stick, and walked towards the door, Margery watched him with eager eyes.

"Good-bye for the time, then," he said, and there was a look in his eyes which repaid Margery for all her anxiety. If he could get out of this mess into which he had been, somehow, involved, she had but little doubt of what the outcome would be.

For a few minutes after his departure Margery sat still in her chair, dreaming dreams of unparalleled delight. But soon she realised that there was work to be done, and that, if she did not wish to be very late at her Bayswater home, she would have to get on with it without delay.

The letters which had to be typed, she rushed off at top speed, and signed them with the usual cabalistic scrawl which, in all but the most important letters, she was permitted to use in place of Cook's neat little signature. The list of names and addresses which she had spent most of the day in compiling, she carefully placed in a drawer of her desk, so that she could get on with them the next day.

Then, her work done, she went to the peg where hung her hat and coat, and prepared to leave the office. Adolphus had long ago gone to his home, and was, no doubt, enjoying a hearty tea at this moment, and regaling his wondering family with the fact that he had that day talked with a real, live detective from Scotland Yard.

Somehow, Margery felt amazingly happy. That John Cook loved her, she felt very sure. And, after all, what did all these horrible murder cases have to do with him? He would be able to get away from the awful business before long, and then they would be happy at last.

But as she went to the door, she had yet another shock. It opened slowly, and the now familiar face of Shelley looked in.

"Is Mr. Cook still here?" he asked.

"No, Inspector," she said, "he went home some time ago."

"How long ago?" he asked brusquely. Shelley seemed to have lost his habitual good manners.

"I should think it would be about five o'clock that he left the office," she said, "and I was just going myself. There were a few things that I wanted to clear up, and I stayed on to get them done."

"Does Mr. Cook usually clear off as early as five o'clock?" pursued the detective.

"Now that you mention it, I don't think he does," said Margery, wondering where these enquiries led, "but then, he has very irregular hours."

"So I should imagine," said Shelley.

"But why do you ask these things?" said Margery.

"I don't know whether I can answer that question just yet," said Shelley, "but could you let me have Mr. Cook's home address?"

"Certainly," said Margery, and gave it to him without more ado.

"Thank you." said Shelley, and added, "I think that you will understand the reason for these enquiries later on, Miss Latimer. At the moment I can tell you no more. I'm sorry to be so secretive, but a Scotland Yard man can't afford to tell everything, even to those who are his friends, and have been perfectly frank with him in the past." And with this last shot, he left.

Margery sat down for a moment, wondering what it could all be about. Surely they could not be so closely on John's track, surely they weren't going to arrest him right away. Her heart went cold at the thought.

Presently, however, she strolled into the street, and made for the Underground Station, *en route* for home. As she passed the newsstand at the entrance to the Station, a flaming placard caught her eye.

"ANOTHER MOTOR MURDER!" it said. Margery fumbled in her handbag, produced a penny, and bought a paper. Hurriedly she glanced over its columns, at last finding what she was looking for.

We understand [the report said] that Mr. Victor Dunn, the managing director of Dunn, Benson & Co., the manufacturers of the well-known "Dunn-Benson Six," the famous racing-car, was found stabbed in his home at Slough at five-thirty this evening. No details are yet forthcoming, but it is believed that the police have a clue to the murderer, which they are following up. Inspector Shelley, of Scotland Yard, has been called in, and an arrest is imminent. This murder will recall to the minds of our readers the remarkable fact that two other men, prominently associated with speed-racing, Sir Henry Henshaw and Lord Chaney, were also murdered in mysterious circumstances a few weeks ago.

Margery stood there for a moment, and she almost felt her cheeks pale. So that was why Shelley had been enquiring about the time when John Cook left his office. So that was the reason for Shelley's remarkable reluctance to tell her anything about it.

And then there came a more horrible thought still. At Slough, the paper said, and at five-thirty! Margery did a piece of rapid mental arithmetic, thought of the time that it would take Cook to get from Chancery Lane to Paddington, from Paddington to Slough. Could it be done in half an hour? If he were lucky enough to catch a quick connection at Paddington, it seemed quite possible. And if so, she might be helping to put a rope around the neck of the man she loved!

Like someone in a dream, Margery stepped on to the escalator, and was carried down to the train which was to take her to Bayswater.

CHAPTER VI

THE THIRD MURDER

"If you can spare me a few minutes, Mr. Bellingham," said Inspector Shelley, "I should be much obliged. I think that you may have some information which will be very useful to me, very useful indeed." The two men were in Mr. Bellingham's office in Chancery Lane, and it was the morning following the discovery of the murder of Victor Dunn.

"Anything that I can do to help you, I will," said Bellingham, "you know that, I imagine, without my saying it, Inspector. This murder of poor Dunn has meant a lot to me. Apart from the fact that I knew him personally, he was a very valuable client, and I shall miss the money which his business brought. That, of course, is between ourselves."

"Oh, quite so," Shelley reassured him, "but what I really want to know now, is this: when did you see Mr. Dunn last?"

"That is what makes it so peculiarly painful," said Bellingham, "I was at his house in Slough yesterday afternoon—in fact, I am not at all sure that I was not the last man to see the poor fellow alive."

"Except the murderer," said Shelley, with that grave smile of his.

"Except the murderer, of course," added Mr. Bellingham.

"Well," said Shelley, "and why did you go down there? I need not tell you, Mr. Bellingham, that any information which you give me will be quite confidential. Scotland Yard does not make public more information than is necessary, you know, but it is essential that we get at the solution of these crimes somehow—and that the death of Dunn has some connection with those other murders of some weeks back, I am very sure."

Bellingham paused for an appreciable time before replying. He was clearly in doubt as to whether it would be wise to take the detective fully in his confidence. At last, however, he took the plunge.

"I hope that it won't be necessary to make these details public," he said, "but you, of course, must be the judge of that. At any rate, this is what happened. Dunn was negotiating a merger with another large motor firm—I'll give you their name, if you want it—and he was rather suspicious of their methods. He thought, in fact, that he was being swindled in some way over the deal. There was, of course, a solicitor who specialises in such work who was really in charge of the business, but Dunn asked me to run through the agreement with him, and see if there was a loophole left anywhere."

"What was the trouble?" Shelley was deliberately laconic. He did not want to interrupt the flow of narrative more than was absolutely necessary. He knew, only too well, how a man who was telling a story which, in his heart of hearts, he felt unwilling to relate, might be made to stop suddenly, if much interruption came.

Bellingham paused and thought again.

"Well," he said at last, "actually, there was, as far as I could see, nothing wrong, but then, as I said, I am not a specialist in such work. I think that Dunn only asked me to look at the agreement because I was his own solicitor, for his private affairs, and a personal friend of his, as well."

Shelley nodded. He could understand that a man who thought he was being swindled by his business associates would hesitate to say so to any but the most discreet solicitor.

"But what did Dunn imagine was the matter?" he asked.

"I think he thought that they were arranging to palm off on him some more or less worthless shares," answered Bellingham, "you know, of course, that when these mergers are carried out, usually little money passes hands. It is largely a question of allotting shares in the new company which is to be formed between the shareholders of the two old ones. Well, Dunn thought that the other company was trying to 'do' him over it, to use the vulgar phrase."

"But there was nothing in the suggestion?" Shelley's remark was really more of a statement than a question.

"As far as I could see, no," said Mr. Bellingham.

"Well," pursued Shelley, "I'm afraid that I shall have to ask you for the name of the other firm, Mr. Bellingham."

"You will keep it quite dark?" said Bellingham, "you won't let the faintest suggestion of it get out, will you? I don't know what the effects would be on the Stock Exchange, and I hold a few shares in both companies. I'm not anxious to see them go down to next to nothing, you know."

"You can rely on me," said Shelley, with a smile, "Scotland Yard is nothing if not discreet in little matters like this, you know."

"Very well," said Mr. Bellingham, "the other firm was the Locke-Macdonald combine."

Shelley whistled gently. The famous "Locke Straight Eight," which had won every trophy of the motor world, was well known to every motor enthusiast, and he saw what a stir would be created by a merger between the makers of this well-known car, and the almost equally famous Dunn, Benson & Company.

There was another surprise awaiting him, however. He had only one more question to ask, he did not expect a satisfactory answer to it, and he was, therefore, all the more amazed at the answer he obtained.

"One thing more, Mr. Bellingham," he said, "whilst you were at Slough, did you see anyone you knew to be an acquaintance of Mr. Dunn's?"

"I've been rather wondering what answer I should make if I were asked some such question as that, Inspector," said Bellingham, "and I can only give you my impression of the matter. Dunn's house, where I expect you've been, is in Albert Square, a hundred yards or so behind the High Street at

Slough, and as I was coming away from the house, walking towards the station, to catch my train back to London, I saw a man slink around the other corner—further from the main road—whom I thought I recognised."

"At what time was this?" asked the detective.

"Oh, about a quarter of an hour past five," said Bellingham, and the detective stared at the curious turn of phrase, "and I can be certain about that, as I hurried to catch the five-thirty train to town."

"Yes, Mr. Bellingham," said Shelley, "and who was this man whom you recognised?"

"I only said that I thought that I recognised him," returned the other, "and I should not like to swear to it. I am the last man to wish to do another an injury, and I can only give you my impressions for what they are worth."

Shelley wished that this tedious old man would hurry on with his description. "Who was the man?" he asked.

"I think—mind you, I only say I *think*" said Bellingham, "that it was my friend, John Cook!"

As Shelley walked along Chancery Lane, to visit the Holborn offices of the Locke-Macdonald Company, Limited, he had plenty of food for thought. Was the old man telling the truth? He had certainly been frank enough about his visit to Dunn, but then, he would know that the police would find out all about that from the servants at Slough, as, in fact, they had. Williamson, the dead man's butler, had testified that he had admitted Mr. Bellingham to see his master at a time which he estimated at from half-past three to four. He had also let the visitor out at five-fifteen. It all agreed very well with Bellingham's own story. But suddenly, a thought struck Shelley. He went into a telephone booth and asked for the number of Dunn's house at Slough, first hurriedly looking at the money in his pocket, to see if he had the necessary change for the phone call.

"Is that Williamson?" he asked, when at length he got through to the house.

"Yes, sir," said the deep voice of the servant, "who is that?"

"This is Detective-Inspector Shelley," he said, "you remember our conversation last night?"

"Yes, sir," said Williamson.

"Well, Williamson, there is one little point which I want settled," said Shelley, "you remember that you told me about a visitor whom you admitted to your master yesterday evening? Mention no names, please. There is such a thing as tapping telephone wires."

"I remember the visitor in question, sir," said Williamson, as ever the soul of discretion.

"Did you actually see your master as or after this visitor left?" asked Shelley, "or was he dead when you next saw him?"

"I saw and spoke to Mr. Dunn after the visitor had left, sir," said the butler, "he asked me to get some cigarettes and fill the box in his study, which was empty."

"Thank you," said Shelley, "that's all."

That at any rate, he thought, as he left the booth, disposed of one possibility. He had suddenly wondered whether, after all, Bellingham might not be lying about his visit, whether, after all, Dunn were not dead when Bellingham had left him. But Williamson's testimony disposed of that possibility.

Williamson had spoken to Dunn after Bellingham had gone, and, about half an hour later, had gone into the study to find his master lying across his desk, the knife of the murderer sticking in his back. So that was that. What was he to do next? Well, the first thing was obviously the errand on which he was bound: these Locke-Macdonald people must be sounded about this precious merger scheme of theirs. It did not seem a very likely plan of attack, but every avenue must be explored. And then, when he had finished with them, Mr. John Cook would have a stern "grilling," as they call it in the States. After all, he had been either on the spot or very near it when all three murders had been committed, and that was a fact that took some getting around.

Shelley was loath to admit it, but John Cook was in a tight corner. And the detective was sorry, for he had a warm spot in his heart for the young man, and found something very likeable about him. There was nothing extraordinary about that, however, even if he was a murderer. Shelley remembered the last murderer he had arrested, a young man from out Balham way, who had been as pleasant-spoken a fellow as you could hope to meet.

He told himself, however, that he mustn't be too previous about the matter. John Cook might be guilty or not. For the moment he had to try to keep an open mind about it, and see what these Locke-Macdonald people could tell him about the suggested merger. That he would have to handle them very carefully, he knew. Stock Exchange people were very touchy, if there was any possibility of their secrets leaking out: and a firm which was negotiating a merger came, for all practical purposes, within the realm of Stock Exchange people.

He soon arrived at the palatial premises of the Locke-Macdonald Company, Limited, in Holborn, where there is always a show of the elaborately-designed and luxurious cars in which they specialise, on show. The company, starting in America to out-Ford Ford, and provide luxury cars for the million, had, at any rate as far as its British sister company was concerned, concentrated on providing two-thousand pound cars (or what looked like two-thousand pound cars) at prices nearer five hundred pounds, and Shelley could not resist waiting for a moment in the doorway of the showrooms and admiring the stream-lined models which were on exhibition there.

"I want to see the manager, please," he said to the stylishly-dressed salesman who came forward to greet him.

"Yes, sir," said the man, "and what name shall I say, please? The manager is very busy, but he always tries to attend personally to people's wants, when they ask for him."

"It's not the manager of the sales department that I want," said Shelley rudely, "it's the manager of the company. I'm a detective from Scotland Yard, so look sharp, young man." And he handed him an official card. Shelley knew when to exert his authority, and the look of deference which at once came over the salesman's face showed him that he had not mistaken his man.

Soon he found himself in the neat little office which was the business home of Mr. Bruce-Smith, the managing director of the company, and he settled himself down in the comfortable armchair which was offered him, and prepared to get the information he wanted.

"I'm here, sir," he began, "in the course of my investigations of the death of Mr. Dunn, of Dunn, Benson & Company."

"But what's that to do with us?" asked Mr. Bruce-Smith, with a lift of his expressive eyebrows, "they're business rivals of ours, of course, but one doesn't usually settle the hash of a rival firm by stabbing its principal."

"Information has come to me," said Shelley stolidly, "that gives me to understand that your firm were contemplating a merger with Dunn, Benson & Company, and I want to know what you can tell me about it."

"Not so loud, please, Inspector," implored the managing director, "if that information gets out, no one can tell how the stock market will take it. You will keep it secret, won't you, Inspector?"

"I can make no rash promises, sir," said Shelley, "but I can assure you that I will do my best to see that this information does not leak out prematurely."

"And what do you want to know, Inspector?" asked the other.

"Anything that you can tell me about the suggested merger, sir," was Shelley's reply.

Mr. Bruce-Smith thought for a full minute before answering, and his pencil traced aimless designs on the scribbling-pad which lay before him on his desk.

"I can only say this, Inspector, which you apparently do not know already," he said, "and I also want you to keep it a close secret as long as you possibly can. The suggested deal was not a merger in the accepted sense of the word, although the markets would have been told that it was. I am not at all sure that what it had been proposed to do was not sailing very close to the law, so you can see that I am trusting you in giving you this information."

"And, if you don't mind my cutting into the conversation, what is this very valuable information at which you are hinting, sir?" interrupted Shelley.

"Oh, yes," said the managing director, recalled back to the main thread of his argument, which he had been forgetting, "well, the fact of the matter is that the firm of Dunn, Benson & Company was on its last legs. We were, not to put too fine a point on it, buying them out, lock, stock and barrel. But Dunn was such a confoundedly touchy chap that he wouldn't have it said that he had been compelled to sell to the highest bidder, and so he arranged that it should be described as a merger, and made to look like one."

"But what about the shares which he was to be given in the new company?" objected the detective, "for that, I understand, is the way that a merger is usually arranged."

"We should buy them back from him at a nominal price," the other told him, "and he would only be permitted to hold a small number."

"Well, is that all that you have to tell me about this suggested deal?" he asked at last, "are you sure, Mr. Bruce-Smith, that you have given me all the information which is available?"

"Good heavens, what more do you want?" said the man, "what I've told you already is enough to finish my business career if it's ever made public."

"Do you know anyone who would gain by Mr. Dunn's death, for instance?" asked the detective.

"Nary a one," said Bruce-Smith, "we shall lose, to the extent that the goodwill of Dunn's will not be ours, for I don't expect that the deal will go through, now. The shareholders of Dunn's will certainly lose, for we were to buy them out at par—the debenture-holders, I mean. Dunn held all the ordinary shares himself."

"And who gains?" the detective was speaking to himself rather than to his companion.

"No one, as far as I know," said Bruce-Smith, and with that Shelley left him.

He walked along Holborn in a rank bad temper. Every line that he started working on seemed to peter out. It was the Henshaw case over again. Then he had worked on two or three things that looked promising, and they came to nothing at all in the end. And now the same sort of thing was happening.

Still, he would see whether John Cook could tell him anything about it. He hurried down Chancery Lane again, and along Fleet Street, reflecting as he went how curiously all the various threads of this very tangled skein seemed to be associated with a very small area. Chancery Lane, Fleet Street, Holborn—they were all within a stone's throw of each other. And the various people, several of whom knew more than they would tell, were all to be found within this tiny piece of London. It made the case look simpler than it was, that was the only trouble. And his chief at the Yard would expect him to finish off the job in no time. "The thing's easy, Shelley," he would say, "there are the people, all of 'em clustered together. Pay your money and take your choice, but for heaven's sake don't be long about it." Oh, Shelley knew exactly what would be said. And he knew that there were strangely tangled threads beneath the whole affair, threads which would take a long time in the unravelling.

But he did not anticipate one of the threads which he found, when he arrived at Crane Court and enquired of the youthful Adolphus whether he could see Mr. Cook.

"I'll ask Miss Latimer, sir," said Adolphus, and vanished into that lady's office.

"Will you see Miss Latimer, sir?" he enquired, a little later, emerging excitedly.

"Oh, I'm so glad you've come, Inspector," said Margery, "I'm awfully worried, and I think that you'll be able to help me."

"What's the trouble, then, Miss Latimer?" said Shelley, kindly.

"Mr. Cook hasn't come in today," she said.

"I expect he's got a cold or something," Shelley told her reassuringly, "or else he's got some important business on elsewhere. He didn't have time to let you know, perhaps."

"I'm sure it's not that," she said, "because once or twice before, when he hasn't been able to come, he's always let me know about it. And besides I've rung up his house, and he didn't come home last night. Mr. Shelley, Mr. Cook has disappeared, and you have got to find him!"

CHAPTER VII

WHERE IS COOK?

DETECTIVE - INSPECTOR SHELLEY was annoyed. He did not often permit himself the luxury of anger, but now he felt that he deserved to be allowed to let himself go. Here was the man who had quite possibly committed three of the most brutal murders of recent years and he had just calmly vanished into thin air. The thing was the worst piece of bad luck which he had encountered for years—and the papers were talking.

Every man who aspires to high rank at Scotland Yard has to get accustomed to newspaper criticism. After all, slack seasons will occur, seasons when there is no really sensational news to report, and then a tired editor can always fall back on the old, old, stunt of "Twenty Unsolved Murder Mysteries in the Past Six Months!" (Newspaper editors, it is well known, think in headlines.)

This, at any rate, is what Shelley was thinking that day as he sat in his chair at Scotland Yard, and mused over the case. It had, he thought, been abominably mismanaged, and the Commissioner would probably have something to say about it before very long.

With a savage gesture he pressed the bell-push on his desk before him, and ordered the uniformed constable who entered to find out if Sergeant Cunningham was in yet.

"I saw him as I came up the stairs, sir," said the constable, "he had just come in, I think."

"Find him, and send him to me, then," snapped Shelley, in a worse temper than ever. He fancied, somehow, that he saw the ghost of a smile hovering over the policeman's face. Make fun of his failures, would they? He'd show 'em!

Soon, however, his anger had a chance to vent itself. Sergeant Cunningham was the man who should have traced the missing John Cook, and had, in some unaccountable manner, failed to do so. Shelley was a fair enough chief as a rule, but, in his present temper, he was unable to help himself.

"Well, what have you got to say for yourself?" he growled, as Cunningham entered.

"I'm sorry, sir, but I don't see how it could have been helped," said the Sergeant obstinately.

"You don't eh? Well, answer this: did I or did I not order you to keep a close watch on John Cook's house at Hampstead?" As Shelley asked the question his eyes flashed a message of anger at his subordinate. Cunningham knew that the Inspector in this mood was a nasty man to cross.

"You did, sir, and I carried out orders," he said.

"Well, how did you lose the man?" asked Shelley, "how on earth did you lose him, now, quick?"

"I lost him, sir, because I am afraid that I scared him off. You see, I only had a photograph to go by, never having set eyes on the man in my life, and when he came around the corner and saw me, for a minute or so I didn't quite realise who he was."

"Fool!" was Shelley's only comment

"Well, sir, that's as it may be, but he turned around in his tracks, and made off down the street as fast as he could go. He didn't try to get into the house, of course, and I wasn't at all sure that it was really our man."

"What time did all this happen?" Shelley was cooling down a little now, his anger slowly evaporating. He was beginning to realise that the Sergeant had done his best.

"Seven o'clock, sir, or as near as possible."

"Well, it's all damned bad luck," said Shelley, "but I suppose that we'll have to put up with it. Until I learned from Miss Latimer this morning that Cook had disappeared, I imagined that you and Pinto between you had kept tabs on Cook. I was intending to go down and arrest him right away. Now I shall have to wait awhile before I have that pleasure."

"Do you think that he did the murders, sir?" Sergeant Cunningham was interested, absorbingly interested.

"I've not altogether made up my mind on that point, Cunningham," said Shelley thoughtfully, "but I am sure that that young man knows a darned sight more than he's told us. And I have an idea that a night spent in the cells might make him talk. Still, we shall have to wait a bit before we try that out. Now, where's the young man live?"

"Eight, Bishopston Row, Hampstead," said the Sergeant, and explained further, "it's one of those little houses just off the Heath, sir. Not common, you know—in fact, far from it—but small and neat."

"I see. Live alone?" Shelley was now in one of his less talkative moods, and the Sergeant fell in with it.

"Yes, sir," he said, "stays in the city for most meals, I understand, and can manage to fry an egg for his breakfast when he wants one. He has a woman who comes in one or two days a week to clear up, but except for that no one is seen there from one year's end to another."

"Well, Sergeant," said Shelley, getting up from his chair and reaching for his hat, "this is your pigeon and you may as well watch the killing of it. In other words, I could bear to see the interior of Eight, Bishopston Row, Hampstead, and I want you to come with me."

Soon they were speeding through London in one of the Yard's most expensive cars, and it was not long before the driver drew up near the famous expanse of Hampstead Heath.

"This is the place, sir," he said, and Shelley thanked him.

"Now, Cunningham," he said, as they walked slowly up the path towards the tidy little villa, "this is where you look discreetly the other way." Cunningham grinned expressively as Shelley drew from his pocket a queer-looking arrangement of wires. Shelley tried this on the lock of the front door for a moment, muttering, "Hope there's no bolt. If so, we'll have to get round to the back."

There were sundry grunts and suppressed exclamations, but it was not more than a minute and a half before the door was open before them.

And then a thought suddenly struck Shelley. What had Margery Latimer said? "I've rung up his house, and he didn't come home last night." That was it, wasn't it? Then who answered the phone?

"What days does the woman who does the cleaning come in?" he asked suddenly. Cunningham looked surprised, but answered readily enough.

"Mondays and Thursdays, with an occasional Friday," he said.

"Then don't go on with your search, until I've phoned," said Shelley, "just shut the door and then sit down."

The phone took some finding, as a matter of fact. It was not on the hall table, in any of the recesses of the sitting-room, or in any such ordinary position. Actually, it was only the ringing of the bell that put Shelley on its track. It was inside a cupboard in the kitchen, which had its door locked, but, fortunately, the key in the door, so that it was not necessary for Shelley to do any more conjuring tricks with his wire arrangements.

"Who's that? Is it you, John?" came a woman's voice, as he took the receiver up, and placed it to his ear.

"Who's there?" he said, disguising his voice as best he could.

"John, it's Margery," said the woman, "oh, John, I'm so frightened. Where have you been, and what have you been doing? Why didn't you let me know where you were? Oh, and I must tell you that Inspector Shelley was here. I believe that he knows something about you. I think he's heard about your being there when the Bayswater business was done. John, why don't you answer? Oh, it is John, isn't it?"

With a grim look on his face and grimmer thoughts in his mind, Shelley hung up the receiver. So Margery knew something about it all, did she? "The Bayswater business," indeed! That was a pleasant way for an innocent girl to refer to a murder. And now, who could he trust in this confounded business? He had thought that he would be able to place some reliance on what Margery told him. Of only one thing was he certain. She did not know what had become of Cook. She had tacitly admitted that by her many hurried questions during those few seconds on the phone. And if she did not know where Cook was, she had probably told the truth when describing his disappearance. That was fairly easily settled, anyhow.

He dialled the number of the office of the National Anti-Speed Association. In a moment Margery's voice, tense with anxiety, answered him.

"Miss Latimer," he said, speaking in his ordinary voice, "I want you to answer one question. This is Shelley speaking."

"Oh yes, Mr. Shelley," she said, "I recognised your voice at once. I was always good at recognising voices on the phone." He smiled grimly, thinking that she had not recognised the last voice she heard, anyhow.

"Tell me," he said, "you said this morning that John Cook had not returned home last night. How did you know that?"

She gave a little laugh of surprise. "Is that all you wanted to know?" she asked, "why, that's easy. His man told me, when I rang up this morning."

"His man?" Shelley was puzzled once more. "What is the name of his man?"

"I'm sure I don't know," she said, "but I know that it was his man, because he told me so."

"Who told you so?"

"Why the man, of course." Again she laughed, and then apologised. "I should be ashamed of myself laughing when Mr. Cook may be in awful peril somewhere, only, only, well, we did sound rather like a couple of back-chat comedians in a music-hall, didn't we? Anyhow, this is exactly what took place, Mr. Shelley. When I rang up this morning the number which Mr. Cook had told me was his private wire there was no reply for a moment, and then a voice that I've never heard before said 'Who's that?' I told him, and asked for Mr. Cook, and he said, 'I am Mr. Cook's man, miss, and I'm sorry that I can't tell you where he is. I haven't seen him since yesterday morning.' And then he rang off. That's all." She stopped with some abruptness, as if this long speech had exhausted her in some way.

Shelley thought for a moment.

"What sort of voice was it that you heard?"

"Oh an ordinary voice," she said, "I know that sounds stupid but it isn't at all easy to describe a voice unless there's a foreign accent or a stammer or something distinctive like that about it."

"Can't you think of anything which would put me on the man's track?"

"Why?" she asked suddenly.

"Well, I don't see why I should take you into my confidence," he said, "but I will. Mr. Cook has no servant. He lives quite alone. Now do you understand?"

"Then who. . . who. . . who did I speak to?"

He caught himself nodding idiotically at the telephone.

"Exactly," he said, "that's what I want to know. Now can you remember anything about the voice, anything at all?"

"Well," she said slowly, "it was rather a gruff voice, like a workman's voice. I remember thinking that Mr. Cook had rather a queer manservant. He sounded more like a navvy."

"Cockney accent?" asked Shelley.

"Oh yes," she answered eagerly, "he spoke like the stage Cockney. You know, all exaggerated and rough."

"Well," said Shelley, "I'm afraid that won't get us far. But it's something, anyhow." Then he added, as if it were a complete afterthought, "I suppose you haven't heard from Cook since, have you?"

"I?" asked Margery in agitated tones, "I? Why should I? No, of course, I haven't heard from him since. I only wish that I had. There are all sorts of things in the office here which want attending to, and I haven't the foggiest notion of how to deal with them."

"Right," said Shelley curtly, and hung up the receiver with a slam. What was it that the girl was keeping from him? That she knew something about John Cook seemed very sure. But what was it? And who was the man who had been in this house that morning? Who?

It was almost with an air of surprise that he encountered Sergeant Cunningham in the passage.

"I'm afraid we're too late, sir," the Sergeant began.

"Too late? What do you mean?" asked the Inspector.

"This, sir," said Cunningham, and led the way towards the back door, which was along a passage from the kitchen. Shelley wondered what was coming, and was, quite frankly, prepared for anything. He was not, therefore, particularly surprised when he found the back door open.

"Did you find it like this, Sergeant?" he asked.

"Yes, sir," said the Sergeant, "and you see how he got in." He pointed to a broken pane of glass in the door.

"He?" Shelley was determined to dispute every point with this confounded subordinate of his.

"Yes, sir," said Cunningham, and pointed to the muddy path which led from the back door towards the fence in which there was a gate.

In that path there was a confused jumble of footprints, but one set stood out above all the others. It was clearly made recently. It was small, dainty, sharp-toed, but still unmistakably masculine.

"About four or five would be the size of that, Cunningham," said Shelley, "and what size boots does Cook take?"

"Nines or tens, I should think, sir," said the Sergeant, "at any rate, you told me that he was over six feet high."

"M'yes." Shelley was thoughtful again. "Look here, Sergeant, how late did you stay watching this confounded house last night?"

"Until midnight, sir, and Pinto relieved me then," said the Sergeant.

"Did you see this small-footed visitor?"

"No, sir. But then we couldn't watch the front and the back door simultaneously. You only put one man on the job, you know, sir, and he had to skip to and fro, between the front and the back door as well as he could."

"All right, man, all right," said Shelley irritably, "you needn't try to teach me my job. I suppose our friend watched until you—or Pinto—probably Pinto, I should think, left the back door, and then he got in before Pinto found his way around again."

"That's it, sir," agreed Cunningham.

"Is Pinto still on duty?" asked Shelley.

"Yes, sir," said the Sergeant.

"Get him," said Shelley briefly.

But Detective-Sergeant Pinto could not help them. He had seen nothing, heard nothing, although he had been on duty outside the house for the best part of twelve hours.

"All right, Pinto," said Shelley, "you can go off duty now. I expect Cunningham and I will be here for two or three hours at any rate. We shall have to go through this place with a small-toothed comb, to see if we can't pick up a clue of some sort."

Cunningham groaned inwardly. He had seen Shelley's "small-tooth comb" methods before, and he knew what they meant. No chance of getting any lunch, at any rate. He would be lucky, he told himself, if he got any tea today.

As a matter of fact, it wasn't quite as bad as that. But it was bad enough. Shelley thought that he had never seen a house so devoid of what might be called personality. It looked just like what might happen to a man who walked into one of those shops in the Tottenham Court Road, and gave the manager carte-blanche to furnish as he liked. No distinction about the furniture, no books, not even a radio.

And there were mighty few places where things could be hidden. In the sitting-room and in the kitchen they drew blank. There was absolutely nothing at all which even remotely suggested an owner. One would have found more personality in an hotel, Shelley thought, and said as much to Cunningham.

"Yes, sir," said Cunningham, "it is peculiar that there is nothing at all to tell us what sort of a man Mr. Cook is. Like as if he was hiding himself away, sir."

"By Jove!" Shelley was startled. "That may be it, you know, Cunningham. He may not be Mr. John Cook at all. If I wanted to hide myself so that no one knew who or what I was, I should do exactly what Mr. Cook has done. I'd get my house fitted up on the mass-production plan like this, and then no one would know anything about me. It's a great idea, you know."

Cunningham almost blushed. He had not quite intended it that way, but if the Inspector took it that the idea was his subordinate's suggestion, that subordinate was not going to quarrel over it.

"Well, let's hope that we have some better luck in the bedroom," said Shelley, as they trudged up the stairs.

The first room they entered was unused. No furniture, no carpets, no pictures, nothing. It was just like an empty room in an empty house. There was not even any dust or rubbish on the floor, as there usually is in an unused room.

The other bedroom—clearly that which John Cook had used—was furnished with a Spartan simplicity. A washstand in the corner contained a jug of water and a basin. There was a dingy-looking wardrobe which had clearly seen better days, and an iron bedstead, small and uncomfortable-looking. That was all. No pictures, no dressing-table. The contrast with the rooms downstairs was surprising. The rather garishly ordinary furniture which there had met their eyes was only for the benefit of casual visitors. The real John Cook was here revealed.

"Not exactly a man for home comforts, Mr. Cook, was he?" said Cunningham.

Shelley smiled. "No," he said, but I think that we shall get a little more out of this room than we did downstairs."

For a time it looked as if they were wrong. There was nothing which could be regarded, even remotely, as a clue. In the wardrobe there was one solitary suit, looking very much the worse for wear, at which Shelley smiled. "Not exactly the sort of clothes for a millionaire, eh, Cunningham?"

"You think. . ." The Sergeant hesitated.

"I think," said Shelley, "that Mr. John Cook was not exactly the meek and mild gentleman which we thought him. This suit looks more like a disguise than anything else. And so"— he added—"does this." He pounced on the floor, near the washstand, and picked up what Cunningham thought looked like a piece of fluff.

"What is it, sir?" he asked.

"My dear Cunningham!" said Shelley, in shocked tones, "do you mean to tell me that you have been at Scotland Yard for all these years, and don't know false hair when you see it? At least, I don't exactly mean false hair, for this is real hair. I mean a part of a false beard!"

That was the sum total of their discoveries in the house, with one notable exception. The exception was a discovery of Cunningham. As they were leaving he suddenly thought of the ash-bin. He thought that his chief always insisted on going through the ash-bin. After all, the things which had been thrown away were often the most important of all.

And in the ash-bin, with the usual mess of discarded pots and pans, empty sardine-tins and worn-out brushes, he found it.

It was a small piece of paper, on which was written: "Victor Dunn, 6, Albert Square, off High Street, Slough."

CHAPTER VIII

THE STRANGER

WHILST Shelley was fretting himself over the latest developments of the case, and trying to track down John Cook, Margery Latimer was trying, in her way, to find where that elusive young man had gone.

She had many motives for this. For one thing, she was quite sure that he would not have disappeared voluntarily without letting her know something about his whereabouts. In the new state of their relations, that, at any rate, seemed unthinkable. And if that was admitted, it meant that he had not disappeared voluntarily. Therefore, he had either been kidnapped, for some unknown reason, or—she hardly dared formulate the thought to herself—he had been murdered! There was a steady accumulation of work at the office, too. Despite the fact that most people were disposed to think of this National Anti-Speed Association as the wildest lunacy, there were a large number who thought it a very sound idea. There were letters arriving by every post, answers to the cunningly-worded little advertisements which John had put in the personal columns of all the principal newspapers; there were answers to the appeals which he had sent to every member of the House of Commons, on the subject of deaths caused by excessive speed on the roads; there was even a letter of thanks signed, personally, by the Minister of Transport himself, asking for the favour of an interview with John. For this was the year during which all sorts of experiments were tried out by the said minister, in the vain effort to stem the rising tide of accidents on the public highways of England, which threatened to do more damage to the populace than any war which had ever been.

But Margery let all these things slide. She had only one thought—to find John Cook. When, for one wild moment, she had thought that she was speaking to him on the telephone, she gave herself away badly. She realised that only too well, but she had no idea who it could be who was at his house. She had no idea where that house was. It was certainly not under his name in the telephone directory, and yet someone had been there! And someone had been there this morning, too, but she felt sure that it was not the same man.

Inspector Shelley had told her that Cook had no servant. Who could it be? Margery pressed her hand to her aching brow in a vain effort to ease the throbbing which threatened to destroy her very ability to think. Where was John Cook?

It was at this moment that the telephone bell rang. Margery hurriedly seized the receiver, and listened.

"Is that you, Margery?" asked a voice.

"It is Margery Latimer speaking," she said, "who are you?"

"Don't you know my voice?" said the man, "this is John."

Margery gasped. It was all right then. John was alive!

"I shouldn't have known your voice," she said, "but then voices sound so different on the telephone."

"They do," he replied curtly, "and besides I have to speak quietly, for fear that they will hear me. Now listen, Margery. Do you know the South Kensington Underground Station?"

"Yes."

"Then I want you to come along there right away. Don't tell anyone where you're going. You may be followed by a Scotland Yard man—I dare say you will be—but that doesn't matter. Give Adolphus the day off, and come right along now. Leave the office unlocked. I have lost my key, and may want to get in there later in the evening. But come to the South Kensington Station right away. I will meet you in the entrance." And he rang off.

For a moment Margery hesitated. Was it a trap? She did not very well see how it could be. The man did not sound very much like John Cook, but then, as she herself had remarked, voices sound so differently on the telephone. There was, indeed, only one thing which made her doubtful. Why had he told her to leave the office door unlocked? The reason he gave—that he might want to get in later in the evening—was nonsensical, for might he not have borrowed her key from her when they met?

Anyhow, there was no harm in leaving the door unlocked, for there were no valuables which might be stolen. The safe contained nothing of any value—John himself had told her that—and there was never any loose cash lying about, except the petty cash in the drawer of her desk. And she knew that that did not amount to more than a pound or thirty shillings, all told.

So, after a few moments' thought, she decided that she would have to go. She told Adolphus that there was nothing more to be done that afternoon, and gave him the rest of the day off. Adolphus, knowing that the local cinema near his home was showing the latest gangster product of Hollywood, scurried off to catch a bus, whilst she walked up Chancery Lane to the Underground Station.

In the train she had qualms of misgiving. She had noticed a man in a bowler hat and aggressively becheckered plus-fours who had sauntered slowly along the street behind her, and he was now studying the form of the runners at Ascot in the *Evening Standard*. As he sat directly opposite her, and puffed away at the vile tobacco which filled his briar, Margery watched him. Every few moments he would steal a glance at her. And as they approached each station she noticed that he lowered his paper a little, and looked absently out of the window. But it was at such a point in the window (behind him) that he could watch her reflection, she noticed.

There was no doubt that this was the Scotland Yard man of whom the voice on the phone (she could not think of that speaker as Cook, even now) had spoken. If it were really John Cook whom she was going to meet, she was certainly going to lead Scotland Yard straight on to his track. And Shelley wanted

John Cook very badly. In her mind's eye she could see the detective's hand on Cook's shoulder. She could hear his voice saying, "John Cook, I arrest you for the murder of. . ." But what was she thinking! John was innocent! And here she was at South Kensington. She hurried out of the train, noticing the man with the bowler hat and the plus-fours, dropping his paper and quickly following her.

In the lift, too, he was still there, and as she emerged into the street, she saw that he was still close behind. It was clear that Shelley suspected that she knew more than she would tell, and had put this man on her trail, in the hope that she would lead him to John Cook—which, it seemed, she was doing fairly effectively.

But there was no John Cook! She stood for a moment, irresolute, in the entrance of the station, and then, seeing that he was not there, she sauntered over to the bookstall, and pretended to be very absorbed in the magazines and papers on show.

After awhile, however, she tired of this, and strolled out into the street, looking up and down, as if uncertain of the way to go. It was no good. John wasn't there, and if he had been coming, he would surely, she thought, have been in time to meet her. He had been so emphatic, on the phone, about her coming straight to this station. And now he was nowhere to be seen.

She was never quite sure, later, about how long she waited on that spot. It was, at any rate, a good half-hour, and then she went into a near-by restaurant and had lunch, her attendant partaking of a frugal meal at the next table. Scotland Yard was taking no risks with her, apparently!

Her lunch over, she returned to the station, and looked around again for John, but he was still not in evidence. Presumably he had been unable to come, if that had really been his voice on the phone. By now, she had become very doubtful on that point, but, if it were not John, why had they brought her out here? She had not spoken to a soul since Adolphus had left, and she had been particularly on her guard, lest some attempt at abduction might be made. She did not know what she might be supposed to be aware of, but it was quite possible, if anyone had kidnapped John, that they might think that there was some reason for her being out of the way. But nothing of the kind had happened. No one had tried to get into conversation with her, even.

And no one did so on the way back to Chancery Lane. She simply got out of the train, and walked swiftly up the escalator, followed closely by her detective follower.

The thing was ridiculous. There seemed no reason for the whole episode. She walked slowly up the stairs to the office, her brow creased in thought. What could be the meaning of this affair?

And then, as she opened the office door, she understood. At any rate, she understood in part. The full realisation of the intricacies of the affair was not to come until some time later.

But it was clear why she had been told to go to South Kensington. They had chosen some station a fair distance away to ensure that she would be absent from the office for some time.

That was clear from what she saw now. The office, indeed, looked as if a miniature cyclone had struck it. Chairs were overturned, the seats ripped out. The pictures which had decorated the walls were torn from their frames. The desk was lying on its side, the drawers pulled wildly out, and their contents scattered in indescribable confusion, on the floor. And the safe. . . the safe had a large hole burned in its door, and what had presumably been its contents, including a large address-book and some ledgers, were lying open on the floor in front of it.

Robbery! And then Margery laughed. What fools they were! They must have seen in the papers that John Cook had vanished, and, knowing that he was a very rich man, had taken this opportunity to look in his office and get what they could find. Well, they didn't get much for their money, anyhow.

But then she paused in her mirth. There, lying on the floor before her, was a disproof of that idea. The drawer which had contained the petty-cash was there, the old-fashioned cash-box in which the money had been kept prised open, and the solitary pound-note and few shillings which it had contained, lying peacefully inside it.

It was not robbery, then—or not robbery for mere money. For thieves would certainly take what money there was to be had, even if it were only a pound or so.

Well, there was only one thing to do. She must ring up Scotland Yard. She almost feared to do it, thinking that she might well be bringing the detectives on the trail of John Cook, but this robbery could not go unreported, and, in any case, she felt sure that John was innocent. He might be in an awkward position—had he not said something about a "nasty jam?"—but that Scotland Yard should know the truth at the first opportunity would only be to his advantage in the end.

Shelley was at the Yard, and he promised to come along immediately. In ten minutes he was with her, listening to her tale of what had happened that morning.

"Hoax, evidently," he said, in that laconic way of his, and then, I suppose you can tell me if there's anything missing here, Miss Latimer?"

"Well," she hesitated. "I can tell you all about the things that were in the open here. But I didn't know anything much about the contents of the safe. Nor did I know if there was anything hidden in the pictures or in the seats of the chairs, as our friends seemed to think."

"I don't expect there was anything hidden in that sort of place," he said, "Cook isn't that kind of fellow. But the safe is another matter. It's most unfortunate that you know nothing about that. But it can't be helped. While I am down questioning the people below, Miss Latimer, I wonder if you would mind assisting my Sergeant, and going through all this stuff here? Just let him know if there's anything missing, I mean."

He opened the door to let the Sergeant enter, and she saw, with a twinkling eye, that that gentleman was blushing. The Sergeant—not Cunningham, for that worthy was still on guard at Hampstead—was none other than her friend of the morning, the gentleman of the plus-fours and the bowler hat.

"I expect you've seen the Sergeant before, Miss Latimer," said Shelley, with a grave smile, "but don't let that worry you. We have to keep an eye on everyone concerned in a case of this sort, you know."

"And hope that they will lead you to the principal suspect, I suppose?" she said, with a touch of acerbity in her tone.

"Well, Miss Latimer." Shelley was grim again, now. "You can't say, you know, that you've been completely frank with us. Oh, I'm not complaining," he interposed hurriedly, for she was about to speak, "I know that you have what seem to you good reasons for not telling us everything you know about this case, and with these new regulations, we're not allowed to do anything to make witnesses tell us what they know. But in the meantime it's only business to put a man on your trail."

"Thank you, Inspector," she replied, with the sweetest smile that she could conjure up, "forewarned is forearmed, you know, and I shall take especial care not to do anything which will bring me within the care of the law—at any rate, until your Sergeant, with whom I spent a most amusing morning, is off my track." She wondered, almost as she spoke thus banteringly, how could she so joke when John might be in deadly peril. But somehow she felt sure that he would be able to take care of himself, whatever might be the dangers of his situation.

Shelley left them to it, and went downstairs, where he was fortunate enough to find the caretaker of the block of offices. He was in a little "cubby-hole" (or so Shelley mentally described it) equipped with telephone and all the other necessary adjuncts of his position.

"Tell me," said Shelley, when he had described himself, and mentioned that a robbery had been committed in one of the offices during the midday interval, "can you tell me of any strangers who went up here during that time?"

"I'm afraid I can't," said the man, "I was out from twelve to one. That's my dinner-hour, you see?"

"Yes, yes," answered Shelley impatiently, "but can you tell me of any strangers who went up anytime today, then?"

The man thought carefully. He was maddeningly slow, Shelley thought.

"There was Mr. Jenkins, who has the top floor," he said at length, "there was Mr. Wilkinson, the publisher—he's second floor, there was Mr. Cook—he's first floor, you know—and there was——"

"Stop!" Shelley almost shrieked. "Do you mean to tell me that Mr. Cook went up to his office today?"

"Yes." The man nodded slowly. "That would be about a quarter to twelve, that would. And he come down again about five minutes later. A little man went up just after Mr. Cook come down. Little undersized fellow in a blue suit. That chap is the only stranger I can recall, mister."

To give Shelley's conversation in detail would be tedious at this stage. It will only be necessary to reproduce what he wrote in his note-book. "11.40," he wrote, "Miss Latimer left. 11. 45, Cook (?) enters, leaving five minutes later at 11.50. At 11.55 stranger comes in. 5 feet 5 or 6 inches, small brown moustache, mop of brown curly hair. Blue suit, worn and shiny at the edges, brown trilby hat, brown boots. No overcoat."

That was the sum total of his information. The reason for the query after Cook's name was that, on being pressed, the caretaker was forced to admit that he did not look at the man very closely, taking it for granted that it was Cook.

He had not known that Cook had disappeared, being one

of those people, comparatively common, even in these days, who do not read newspapers, except the sporting column.

But, if it were Cook, why had he come here? And had he really rung up Margery Latimer, in order to get her out of the way before he arrived? If so, why? What had the stranger to do with it? Was he the man with small shoes, whose footprints they had discovered outside Cook's house? If so, what was he doing in this business? The questions were endless, and Shelley's head seemed to spin as he walked up the stairs again to see what Margery had to say.

He was no nearer the solution of this mystery than he had been weeks before, when the murders took place. And the mystery seemed to deepen with everything that happened.

CHAPTER IX

THE MYSTERY DEEPENS

"Now look here, Miss Latimer," said Shelley, "we have got to straighten this thing out somehow. Three murders have taken place. Mr. Cook has disappeared, and now there is this robbery. Can you suggest anything—anything at all— which will explain the connection between all these events?"

Margery shook her head mutely. She had long ago given up hope of reaching any solution of the problem. When she settled down and tried to think the whole thing out, her mind was just a blank: it seemed as if her mind refused to function on this point.

Shelley, it seemed, was in just as bad a state. At any rate, he was at his wits' end to know what to do. The whole problem seemed to have baffled him completely, and, short of finding John Cook, he seemed unaware of any method of getting to the heart of the mystery.

"I'm going to take you into my confidence, Miss Latimer," he said at length, "I want you to keep these ideas of mine quite secret. It is only from you that I can get certain information which is necessary to me."

"Of course," answered Margery, "I shall treat anything that you tell me, in confidence. In any case, I'm not in the way of repeating everything I hear to my friends and acquaintances."

"I know all about that," said Shelley, but you must not breathe a hint of these things to anyone. *To anyone.* I hope that you understand."

Margery understood only too well. John Cook was not to know what the police had found out. That was what Shelley's hints implied. Well, even if she did not tell him about anything which the police told her, there was nothing to prevent her acting on that information, without giving it away, was there? Rather specious reasoning, perhaps, but Margery was in a position where she could not afford to be too finicky about right and wrong.

"I understand, Mr. Shelley," she murmured, "and now, please tell me what it is that you want to know so badly?"

"First of all," said Shelley, producing a grubby piece of paper from his pocket, "do you recognise the handwriting on this?" It was the paper which he had found in Cook's dustbin.

"Of course I do," she answered, without a moment's hesitation, "it's mine!"

"Yours?" Shelley was astonished. "But why should you write down the name of a man who was murdered?"

"Well," said Margery, and she seemed to the detective to be momentarily confused, "you see, he wasn't murdered when I wrote down his name and address. That is one piece out of a list of men connected with the motor trade which I was making out for Mr. Cook. The whole lot, in their final form are filed in a card index which should be somewhere about— if these thieves haven't got rid of it." She looked around for a moment, and finally pounced on a cardboard box which was lying on the floor.

"There," she said, "that's it!" And, looking hurriedly through the hundreds of cards which it contained, she produced one, on which was written: "Victor Dunn, 6, Albert Square, off High Street, Slough. Managing Director, Dunn, Benson & Co." This was in Margery's writing, and beneath, in a strong, masculine hand, there was added: "Shareholder in Associated Armaments, Ltd., Edwards, Bell & Co., and other firms, see vol. xii, p. 197."

"What's the meaning of this entry, Miss Latimer?" said Shelley, pointing to the latter entry.

"Oh, that!" she smiled, "just a little idea of Mr. Cook's. That's his writing, you know. He thought that all these motor firms were in some way linked up with the armament interests, and he made a point of finding out all that he could about the shares which the big motor men held in such concerns. He was fairly successful in showing that they were most of them big shareholders, I believe. Though all that was outside my part of the business. I really had little to do with it: it was Mr. Cook's own private business. The volume he refers to will be found at his house, I think. It's not here, anyway."

Shelley made a note of the fact. These volumes—and there were at least twelve of them—would have to be investigated.

"And now," he went on, "would you be surprised, Miss Latimer, to hear that John Cook was here in this office no later than this morning?"

For a moment Margery stared at him as if he were mad. Then she laughed gently.

"I may not be very old, Inspector," she said, "but I'm too old a hand to be taken in by that old stunt. You can't pull my leg as easily as that, you know." And she laughed again.

"But I was not joking," he replied, "I was quite serious about it. The old caretaker downstairs told me that he saw Mr. Cook—or a man he took to be Cook—coming in this building this morning, about five minutes after you left it."

Margery went deathly pale. For a moment the detective thought that she was going to faint, but by a great effort of will she regained control over herself.

"That can't be so?" she asked. The question was clearly put more to herself than to the Scotland Yard man, but he took it upon himself to answer.

"It not only can be, but it is so, Miss Latimer," he replied as gently as he could, "I assure you that I was surprised when I heard of it. But still I am forced to take the word of the caretaker. He's a decent enough fellow, and anyhow he had no reason to lie about it. He doesn't read the papers—except the racing section—and he didn't know that Mr. Cook was missing."

"Didn't know. It's impossible!" exclaimed Margery.

"It's far from impossible, I assure you," said Shelley, "the number of people who don't read the papers is larger than you would imagine. We at the Yard find that out, when we advertise for some wanted person."

"I'm afraid that I can't help you, Mr. Shelley," said Margery, "this latest development has taken me completely by surprise. I can understand it no better than you can yourself."

At this moment the telephone bell rang, and Margery, who had regained her normal colour by now, picked up the receiver, and, after listening for a moment, handed it to Shelley, with the murmured explanation that the call was for him.

"What?" he shouted into the receiver, after listening for a moment, "another? Right, I'll be there right away."

"Another murder?" asked Margery, "oh, no, it can't be. It isn't another murder, is it, Inspector?"

"Nothing quite so bad as that, Miss," he said reassuringly, "it's another robbery."

"Where? When?" Margery just managed to gasp out these queries.

"At Mr. Cook's house at Hampstead," answered the detective, "I left a man in charge of the house, but he seems to have been overpowered somehow. I must get right along there now. I'll let you know if anything happens, or if I get on the track of Mr. Cook again,"

"Who would be a detective, Cunningham?" he asked some time later, as he walked up the path towards the front door. "Here you've had a pretty nasty smack on the head, and I've had nothing to eat since breakfast. What a life!" And, despite his aching head, Cunningham grinned. The chief was a cheery sort of cove at the best of times. And when you were stumped in the middle of a great case, he had a way of sometimes saying the queerest things.

Soon, however, they were seated at the little table in the sitting room, and Shelley turned abruptly to business.

"Now, what about it, Cunningham?" he asked, "tell me, as quickly as you can, what happened. We must act quickly, or the chap will get away again—if he hasn't got away already, that is."

"Well, sir," answered his subordinate, "after you went, I locked up the front door as you suggested, and sat in the kitchen, facing the passage leading to the back door. There wasn't much to do, and I started reading a paper which I found in this room. This morning's *Daily Mail* it was, by the way, which shows that there was someone here this morning before us."

"We didn't need the paper to prove that, Cunningham," said Shelley, "Miss Latimer told us that she rang up here this morning, and was told that Cook hadn't been home. The man—whoever he was—who told her that, no doubt left the paper behind. But go on."

Cunningham went on. "Suddenly, sir, as I was sitting, glancing at the paper, I heard a sound behind me. It was only a vague sort of noise, but it meant that there was some sort of movement there. I wheeled round in my chair, and, as I did so, someone caught me as nasty a smack on the head as I ever remember getting. That's all, sir. When I came to, I was lying just in the same spot, so the fellow evidently did not want much time, or he would have locked me in somewhere—or at least tied me up."

"Did you ring me up at once?" asked Shelley.

Sergeant Cunningham grinned sheepishly. "As soon as I could drag myself to the phone, sir," he said, "I remembered that you had told me that I should get you either at the Yard or at Cook's office. I rang up the Yard first, and they told me that you had gone out some considerable time before, so I rang up Cook's office immediately and there you were."

Shelley looked thoughtful for a moment.

"Did you catch a glimpse of the man who hit you?" he asked.

"Just the merest glimpse, sir, not more," answered Cunningham. "Certainly not enough to recognise him, if we're ever lucky enough to lay our hands on the sweep!"

"Tall or short?" Shelley was getting curt again.

"Short, sir," he said, "not more than five feet six or seven at the outside, I should say—if I can guess at it from a moment's glance. But quite certainly not more than that. And it can't possibly be Cook himself, sir, if that's what you're thinking."

"I don't know that I was thinking anything in particular," said Shelley, "but in any case I didn't expect that it was Cook. He wouldn't hit a man on the back of the head. At least, I don't think that he's that sort of chap. He might knock anybody out in a straight fight, but that's another matter."

"His face I'm afraid that I didn't see, sir," said Cunningham ruefully, "but then, I only had about one second, I reckon, to see what I did."

"You've done very well, Cunningham," said Shelley, "better than you know, perhaps."

And he told his subordinate of the robbery at the Fleet Street offices.

"The same chap, you think?" asked Cunningham.

"Might be," said Shelley doubtfully, "but that depends largely on how the times compare. What time did he attack you here?"

"One o'clock, as near as doesn't matter," said Cunningham, "I know that, because I was wondering if I should be lucky enough to get anything to eat until teatime. I looked at my watch not long before he came, and it was about ten to one, then."

"He went in the office at five minutes to twelve," said Shelley thoughtfully, "and that would allow him roughly an hour to make a general mix-up of the stuff there, and then come out here and give you a good smash on the head. Yes, he might have done it. And the caretaker at Crane Court said that the stranger there was about five feet five or six. That agrees all right. Of course, we may be on the wrong track altogether. The stranger in Crane Court may have nothing to do with our case at all. He may be just someone who was visiting one of the other offices. I'm advertising for all strangers who visited that block of buildings on that day to come forward. That should straighten things out, anyhow. And in the meantime we've got to fire ahead as well as we can. Have you examined the place to see what's missing?"

"Yes, sir," said Cunningham, "and as far as I can see there is mighty little gone. There was some money in a cash-box upstairs. The box was unlocked and the cash is still there. So it wasn't money that he was after."

"Well," snapped Shelley, "we knew that before, didn't we, fathead?"

"The only thing that I can find missing, sir," said Cunningham, taking the insult without a quiver, for he was used to Shelley's ways, "I should like you to see. It's upstairs, sir."

"Lead the way, then, man!" said Shelley shortly. His temper was obviously on the verge of boiling over. This case was getting badly on his nerves.

Cunningham led the way into the empty bedroom. Shelley was more than a little surprised, but tried hard not to show it. He was, in a way, rather proud of the fact that he never gave away his feelings to those who worked under him. He used to say that it should be the art of the really successful detective not to show that he had any feelings at all. But it is to be feared that he did not always live up to that ideal.

As they reached the bare little bedroom Cunningham paused with a melodramatic gesture.

"There, sir," he said, "what do you think of that?"

The room, at first glance, looked just like it had that morning, when they had looked around. But, in one corner, a floor-board had been prised up, and, scattered around the floor in that corner of the room were a number of small note-books, some with labels on the covers.

How did we miss that this morning, Cunningham?" asked Shelley scornfully. Sergeant Cunningham was grateful for that "we." Shelley, whatever his faults, was always a just man, and would always include himself in the category of blameworthy persons when blame was his due.

"I don't know, sir," said Cunningham, "except for the fact that this board looked as well nailed down as the rest. You'll see, sir, if you examine it, that the nails have been driven through, and then filed off at the back, so that the board had only to be dropped in place for it to look as if it was a proper piece of the floor."

But Shelley was on hands and knees examining the note-books.

The labels of some seven or eight of them bore numbers in Roman numerals. He noted with satisfaction that they ran from VI to XII. Turning to the number XII book, he hurriedly turned the pages. Yes, here was the reference to Dunn, followed by a long list of companies, presumably those in which he had held shares. On the next page, Shelley noted without much surprise, appeared the name of Lord Chaney, whilst a page devoted to the activities of Sir Henry Henshaw was not far away.

A glance at the other numbered books revealed the fact that these, too, were concerned with the shareholding activities of various personages, prominent in the motor world.

That was satisfactory enough, as far as it went. But on turning to the other unlabelled and unnumbered note-books Shelley had a surprise. They were, as far as he could see, absolutely bare of all writing! Simply empty books, in fact.

"Tumbled to it, sir?" said Cunningham quietly, "it took me a good quarter of an hour to realise what had happened."

"What do you mean?" asked Shelley, "have I tumbled to what, you idiot?"

"Count the pages in one of these blank books, sir, and then count the pages of one of the full ones."

Shelley did so, with a growing sense of impatience. This confounded case, he thought, seemed to lead them on to something, and then that something disappeared.

His counting finished, he began to realise what Cunningham had meant. The full note-books contained a hundred pages, the empty ones only sixty. The covers, except for the labels, were identical. The mysterious visitor had torn out forty pages from each of the books. What had been written on those forty pages?

CHAPTER X

A STRANGE VISITOR

MARGERY was not at all satisfied with Shelley's visit. In spite of the fact that he had stated his intention of being frank with her, she was sure that he suspected more than he had told her. Whether he thought John Cook a murderer she had no means of judging, but that he was almost as anxious as she was to find out what had happened to her employer she knew.

She wondered if there were any possibility of her getting on the track of John Cook. It seemed ridiculous, at first sight, to suggest that she should succeed where Scotland Yard, so fair, had failed, but, she reflected, after all she knew John Cook better than the detectives did. She knew his habits, his ways of thought as well as any living person did. It was possible, of course, that he had some purpose of his own, which he had not revealed to anyone, not even to her, but, that apart, it seemed likely that she knew more about his purpose than anyone else.

But where to start? That was the trouble. Margery began to realise the difficulties of a detective's job. The office was more or less tidy again now, for she had spent a busy afternoon after Shelley's departure in putting everything back in its place. Only the gaping hole in the door of the safe remained to bear mute witness to the happenings of the day.

There was only one clue—and this she had come upon after Shelley had gone. It is probable that had she found it before the detective's departure, she would have given it to him. As it was, she felt that she was justified in working on it herself.

It was only a mere slip of paper, this clue. But on it were written some half-dozen telephone numbers, all of them in the London area, and she felt that there might be some vital facts to be obtained from them. None of them were known to her, which seemed to indicate that they were concerned with some secret scheme of Cook's which he had not so far revealed to her.

"Kensington, 71932" was the first number on the list, and she spent a fruitless half-hour trying to find it in the directory. But it is difficult, as many others have found, to discover the address of a person from the telephone directory, when the number is all that is known.

Then she suddenly had a brainwave. Why not ring up the number, and see who answered? The thought no sooner came into her mind than she was putting it into execution.

Pulling the phone towards her with a sudden access of determination, she dialled the Kensington number, and was pleased to hear a female voice reply.

"Kensington 71932," it said, "who is that, please?"

"Who are you?" ventured Margery.

"Kensington 71932," said the unknown, "will you please tell me who you are, and who you wish to speak to?"

"Is Mr. Cook there?" said Margery, drawing a bow at a venture, "if so, I should like to speak to him."

"We have no Mr. Cook here, I'm afraid," said the girl, "I'm sorry, but you are making a mistake. Are you sure that it is Mr. Cook you want, madam?"

"Yes," said Margery, "but I'm afraid that I must be mistaken. I'll enquire again. I must have got the name wrong. Thank you." And she rang off, disgusted with herself for not having obtained any information.

She repeated the manoeuvre with the other numbers in turn. But Battersea 51678, Holborn 55196, Kingsway 88761, Slough 87648, and Windsor 99186 were all equally secretive. In no case did she get any indication of who was speaking. The people at the other end of the wire seemed united in a determination to give no information away, though they were all very eager to know who she was.

She thought deeply for a few minutes when the work was done, and then suddenly a thought struck her. "Slough." What did that recall to her mind? Hurriedly she turned over the leaves of the directory, only to meet with disappointment. "Slough 87648" was not the telephone number of Victor Dunn. She had scarcely hoped that it would be, but it was, at any rate possible. Now that this suspicion was shown to be baseless, Margery was at her wits' end. She could not see where to start. Lost in thought, she was sitting in her chair, her head on her arms, when a voice surprised her.

"Don't move, please, miss," it said, "or you will be very foolish."

Margery looked up with a start, but, before she could turn round she felt the cold barrel of a revolver pressing into the back of her neck.

"Quite still, please," said the voice, "and no turning around."

The situation seemed impossible in the midst of the bustle of modern London, but the compelling urgency of the man's voice was sufficient to assure her that he was in dead earnest.

"I'm afraid, miss," went on the voice, "that I shall have to tie you to the chair, and to blindfold you. I'm really very sorry to give you all this trouble, but I can assure you most sincerely that I have no desire to hurt you in any way. If you obey my orders you shall come to no harm."

The man spoke in a pleasantly cultured tone, although there was something meticulously correct about his phrasing that seemed to indicate the fact that he had not attained to this without an effort. It was rather like the voice of a rather superior servant, she thought. But then, that was ridiculous! What servant would have anything to do with this case?

Anyhow, she was compelled to comply with his demands. There was no other way out.

A handkerchief was tied tightly round her eyes. Then, whilst the man kept up a running flow of reassuring conversation, she was tied, gently but efficiently, to the chair.

"I hope that I'm not hurting you, miss," he said, "but I can't help myself. It won't do for you to give me away to Scotland Yard, you see. I hope that you understand my position."

"What if I scream?" she asked.

"You won't," he said grimly, "I still have my revolver here, and whilst I should be sorry to shoot you—or even to knock you out with the butt, I should not hesitate to do so if I felt that such a course was advisable or necessary for my own safety."

Margery felt an insane desire to giggle, but she kept herself firmly in hand. Hysteria would not help her in her present plight. When the man had first made his entrance she was too scared to scream, and now it was quite clearly too late.

So she sat motionless in her chair, unable to stir a hand. Her arms had been pinioned behind her, and her legs tied tightly to the legs of the chair. This man was no stranger to knot tying, whatever else his conduct might lack.

Strange sounds were emanating from the man. He was grunting to himself, as if in the throes of some intense effort, but presently he gave vent to an exclamation of pleased surprise, as if he had found something for which he had long been seeking.

Margery wondered what he could be doing. Was there something concealed in this office, something which both she and Shelley had overlooked? It certainly seemed so, unless an impossible coincidence had occurred, and there were two sets of people hunting for the same thing. It seemed only too likely that this was the man who had decoyed her away this morning, and then robbed the office. If so, he would be a short man, and, from the way in which he had handled the cords that bound her, she felt sure that he was definitely below the average in height.

In the meantime he was still busily engaged in some mysterious occupation. What it was she could not imagine. He was still grunting at intervals, and she thought that she heard a bump, as if he had deposited some heavy parcel on the desk. But she could not be sure of that. Then he moved around the room, as if making sure that he had forgotten nothing, and finally addressed her again.

"I have to leave you now, Miss Latimer," he said, and she started to hear him use her name. Previously he had merely addressed her as "Miss."

"And how am I to get out of these bonds?" she asked.

"I shall ring up Scotland Yard," he said, "when I am at a safe distance from this place, and inform them of your plight. You will have a little more discomfort to endure. About half an hour or so of it, I should imagine. But my good friend Detective-Inspector Shelley will release you eventually. I need not, I suppose, tell you not to inform Shelley of my appearance—because I did not give you any opportunity of seeing me." And, chuckling at what he evidently regarded as a pleasant little joke, he went off. At least, Margery heard the door close, and then she thought that she heard footsteps going down the stairs. She could not be sure, because the doors were thick—and how thick she had a good means of finding out within the next few minutes.

Giving him a minute or two, just to make sure that he was gone, she proceeded to shout for help as loudly as possible. But not a soul came in answer to her cries. She might as well have been in the middle of the country, she thought, for all the difference her shouting made.

At last, however, the door opened softly, and someone came in.

"Quick," she said, "undo these cords." And the newcomer proceeded, rapidly enough, to do what she asked, not saying a word meanwhile.

Before he had proceeded far, Margery was able to help him, and she was soon free. Then she tore the handkerchief from her eyes to see her rescuer. And this was where she got the biggest surprise of the many which she had endured in the last few days.

Standing before her, a smile on his handsome face, was John Cook!

"John!" she said.

"Margery!" he smiled. And then for a moment all was forgotten, save that she was in his arms.

"Quick!" she said presently, "there's no time to waste. He said that he was going to ring up Scotland Yard. Shelley will be here in no time. You must get away."

"That's a funny welcome for a returned prodigal," he said, "to want to hurry me off again right away." But she could see an anxious look in his eyes as he looked around the room. He was afraid that the intruder had found something. Up to now, he had asked her nothing of the reason for her position: that had, she supposed, been obvious enough. Unless. . . unless. . . but surely John would not alter his voice and tie her up, so that he could get something from this room without her knowing.

"My dear," she said, "don't you see the danger you're in?"

"I see that plainly enough," he said, "but, tell me, did you see anything of the fellow who tied you up? I'm taking it for granted, I might add, that you didn't tie all those beastly knots yourself."

"No," she said, "I saw nothing of him. But, John, you must get away."

"All in good time, Margery," he said, "but for the moment I must find if anything is missing. I've had this place under observation for days, but I didn't dream that you would be hurt. You see, I never suspected that. . . that he was involved in it."

"Who?" Margery could only ask the question. She was wondering if at last the whole truth of this most mysterious affair was to be revealed to her.

"The gentleman who tied you in that chair, my dear," he

said banteringly, "as to his identity, I think it would be safer for you not to know who he was—for the time being, at any rate."

He was prowling round the room all this time, and now he stopped before the door to the inner office, a scowl on his face.

He pointed without a word, and Margery, following the direction of his finger, could see that a board had been lifted bodily from the floor. Something, then, had been taken! And what that something was, she could not guess, but neither Detective-Inspector Shelley nor herself had suspected its presence there.

"Well, I know the worst, anyhow," said John, "he's got it, and it can't be helped now."

"What was there, John?" she asked.

"I'm afraid that once again I must put off telling you that for awhile," he said tantalisingly, "but, you see, the secret is not mine to tell. It's vitally important that nothing of this shall leak out for the time. So I'll beg you to tell Shelley nothing of my little visit when he comes."

"But where have you been?" she asked.

"Ah!" He held up an admonishing forefinger. "Wouldn't you like to know? I've been having a rest cure, if you want to know, Margery. Not that it's been particularly restful, on the whole." Indeed, he looked very tired.

"And when shall I see you again?" asked Margery.

"That," he answered, "is on the lap of the gods. But I hope, Margery, that when we next meet all this fearful tangle will be undone. Then I shall be free to ask you something which I have been wanting to ask you for a very long time."

Margery smiled. She could guess, easily enough, what that question was. They had not been really like lovers to each other, these two, but that first caress, when he had released her from her bonds, showed her more plainly than any words could have done, what he thought of her. And she longed, with all her being, for the day when he should be free from these entangling chains of mystery which seemed to tie him down like a prisoner.

"Good-bye for the time, then," she said, holding out her hand. He seized it in his, pressed his lips to it, and was gone.

Margery settled down to await the arrival of the police, wondering in the meantime what she should tell them. John had said that she should not say he had been there. So she would have to pretend that she had got free of the cords by her own efforts.

It would be a good idea, she thought, to ring up Scotland Yard herself. On her doing so, however, she was informed that Shelley was already on his way, and she had no sooner replaced the receiver of the instrument than the door opened, and the detective burst unceremoniously into the room.

"Thank goodness you're safe!" he said.

"I was in forty fits thinking that you might be hurt. But how is it that you're free? I thought that I should at least find you tied up and gagged."

"I managed to get out of the cords," she said, affecting a weariness which she did not feel, "and there they are."

He picked up the cord with a thoughtful air. Then, with a sudden gesture of urgency, he left the room, to return a moment later with Sergeant Cunningham.

"Cunningham," he said, "do you recognise this cord?"

The Sergeant took up one of the pieces and looked at it intently.

"Yes, sir," he said, "it's unmistakable. That green strand which has somehow got woven in makes it absolutely unique, as far as I know. It couldn't be coincidence, anyhow. The same peculiar stuff wouldn't turn up twice in the one case."

"But where have you seen this cord before, Sergeant?"

asked Margery anxiously.

"I suppose, miss," he replied, "that I ought not to tell you, since our case is a long way from complete. But I will just let you know a little about it, because you're so intimately concerned, so to speak, in the case. This cord, I should be prepared to swear, came from off a big ball of it which we found in the kitchen of Mr. John Cook's house at Hampstead!"

CHAPTER XI

SHELLEY ASKS QUESTIONS

"Now, Miss Latimer," said Shelley, almost before Margery had had time to assimilate this astonishing piece of information, "I think that I shall have, once again, to ask you some questions. I'm afraid that this case is not proceeding as rapidly as we should like—but then, if some of those who should be our principal witnesses refuse to tell us all they know, what can you expect?"

Margery smiled rather self-consciously. The detective was having a little "dig" at her, she felt sure. The reference was only too obviously to herself.

"Carry on, Mr. Shelley," she said, "I will answer your questions—if I can."

"First of all, then," he asked, "will you tell me exactly what happened? Why were you tied up like that? Who did it?"

"I'm afraid that my answers there won't be really very satisfactory, Inspector," she said, "because you see the man came on me from behind. I didn't see him at all, because I was blindfolded with a handkerchief."

"Where is it?" asked Shelley.

"Oh, I expect it's lying about here somewhere," she said, looking around her vaguely.

"Oh, yes, here it is." She stooped and picked up from the floor a dark blue silk handkerchief which looked somehow familiar. She had seen it before, but she could not think where.

Shelley pounced on it and examined it intently. Then he passed it over, without comment, to Cunningham, merely pointing to a tab which was sewn on to the edge of it.

"I suppose that I mustn't ask you to be indiscreet, Inspector?" smiled Margery.

"Meaning . . . ?" said Shelley, his eyebrows raised questioningly.

"Meaning—what is it that you have noticed about that handkerchief?" was Margery's reply.

"Oh, I don't see why you shouldn't see it," said the detective, "after all, it may serve to make you a little more alert about a certain gentleman."

He took the handkerchief back from Cunningham, and passed it to Margery. And, although she was prepared for a rather surprising thing, she could not repress the little cry of astonishment which came to her lips.

The tab which was sewn on the edge of the handkerchief—obviously for the use of a laundry—contained two words. And those two words went through her heart like the stab of a knife, for they were "John Cook." She remembered now, why the piece of silk had been in some way familiar to her: she had seen John Cook wearing it. Always somewhat of a dandy, he had always been proud of having tie, socks and handkerchief to match, and the last time, before today, when she had seen it, it had been in the breast-pocket of his immaculate coat.

"Still sure that you haven't seen Mr. John Cook lately?" asked the detective, and it was only with the utmost effort of will that Margery was able to assure him in a steady voice that she was absolutely certain on that point.

"Well, Miss Latimer," said Shelley, "we must, of course, take your word about it, but the evidence of this handkerchief taken together with the cord, certainly seems to show that Mr. Cook was in this room not long ago. I suppose that your assailant could not be Mr. Cook?"

"Why, of course not," said Margery, "he was a very short man, and Mr. Cook is tall."

"How could you tell that he was short," said Shelley, with an air of triumph in his tones, "if you did not see him at all?"

"But I could feel him, when he was tying me up," said Margery, "and he felt much shorter than Mr. Cook did when—"... She stopped helplessly, realising that she had nearly given away the fact that John had visited her.

She had, indeed, been about to say "Than Mr. Cook did when he untied the ropes." Shelley was quick to seize upon her error.

"Than Mr. Cook did when he was doing what?" said he. "Mr. Cook has been here, then."

"No, no, no!" exclaimed Margery vehemently, "he has not been here. I was going to say that the man who tied me seemed shorter than Mr. Cook did when he came over to my desk and put his hand on my shoulder one day. It was when he wanted to call my attention to a mistake in a letter." The story was pitifully lame, she knew, but she had to cover up her mistake somehow, and the fact that she was blushing furiously did not, she was sure, make her explanation any the more convincing.

"So you can tell, by the mere touch of a man's hand on your shoulder, if he is short or tall," Shelley commented, in that coldly sarcastic tone which, in its time, had cast fear into the heart of many a malefactor. "Most remarkable, Miss Latimer, most remarkable. I suppose that you are not a psychic subject, by any chance, with mediumistic powers."

Margery smiled wanly. "There is a difference, you know," she said, "when a man is definitely leaning down to touch you, and when his arm is more or less level with your shoulder."

"Quite possible," was Shelley's comment, "but I did not know that the man we are looking for was about four feet to four feet six. That would be his height, I think, if his arm, stretched out straight from his shoulder, would be level with your shoulder when he was standing and you were sitting. Better make a note of that, Cunningham," he added, "and remember that the gentleman that we are looking for is a dwarf. It will be easy enough to find him, anyhow. Can't be so many murderous dwarfs about."

Margery writhed under this onslaught. She had brought it on herself, she knew, by that foolish slip in the first instance. But she could not allow Shelley to go on misconstruing her in this way.

"I do not mean to imply that he was as small as all that, Mr. Shelley," she expostulated. "I was only giving that as a sort of example. The man was a little man, I am sure, but not so little that you could call him a dwarf. Say five feet six or so. That would be about his height, I should think. I may be quite wrong, of course," she hastened to add, "but I don't think that I am."

"You didn't catch even a glimpse of him," pursued the detective, "you were blindfolded before you had a chance to see anything at all, weren't you?"

"I was," she replied, "you see, he came up behind me. He must have come in through the other door, that leads direct into Mr. Cook's room from the corridor outside."

Shelley nodded. "What was the first indication you got that there was a stranger in the room?" he asked.

"I didn't know he was there until he spoke to me," said Margery, and detailed the conversation of the stranger, and the subsequent events, omitting only to tell of John Cook's visit.

"And do you think he stole anything?" asked the detective. His eyes had already been roaming the room, and the board which had been raised from the floor had not escaped his notice.

"Something from there, I imagine," she said, and pointed towards the place. Instantly Shelley was on his knees beside the hole.

"Same stunt, you see, Cunningham," he said, holding up the board to his subordinate's notice, and calling his attention to the fact that the nails had been filed off at the undersurface.

It did not take him long, however, to realise that there was nothing to be learnt here. The cache, whatever it had once contained, was now empty. There could be no real doubt about that.

"I'm afraid, Miss Latimer," he said, rising from his knees, and dusting his trousers with a meticulous hand, "that I shall have to get all the boards in this room taken up. You never know, there may be something else hidden here, if so we must find it before our friend gets on the trail once more."

"Is that all for the present, then, Mr. Shelley?" asked Margery anxiously.

"I think it is," he said, with a smile, "unless, anything else occurs to you."

Margery shook her head. She had nothing more to tell.

"Well, then, we will leave you for the present," he said. "I should think that you will be very pleased to get something to eat. After all, you've had a very worrying day. But if anything occurs to you later—anything at all, mind—which seems to have some bearing on the case, I hope that you will ring me up at Scotland Yard right away. If I'm not in, they will be able to get in touch with me without wasting time. And remember, even if it's something which seems to you unimportant, it may actually be of vital importance to us. So don't forget."

"I won't forget," Margery promised, and shook his hand gratefully. After all, even if he had unjustifiable suspicions of John, she thought, he was only doing his job, and it had to be admitted that John was behaving in a very suspicious manner. That handkerchief, for instance, and the cord. Was it possible that it had been John who had tied her up, only to return a little later and restore her to freedom? She shook her head impatiently at the thought, and began to put away her things. It was certainly, as Shelley had suggested, time for a meal.

"Where now, sir?" Cunningham had asked as they emerged into the bustle of Fleet Street.

"Well," said Shelley thoughtfully, "I could bear to know a little more about our good friend Cook. Mr. Bellingham might be able to give us a spot of information. As far as we have found out, he is the only person who knew anything about the gentleman. He got Miss Latimer her position in that office, and he would, presumably, have made sure that Mr. Cook was a respectable sort of fellow before recommending the lady who had been his ward to go there. Anyhow, we shall see more about that in a few minutes."

They were strolling along Chancery Lane while this conversation was going on, and Cunningham was thinking deeply.

"What do you think of Miss Latimer, sir?" he asked, at length.

"Ah, there you have me," said Shelley.

"I'm really not at all sure what I do think about her. She's hiding something—that's very clear. Notice how confused she got about Cook's having put his hand on her shoulder? I should be willing to bet an even fiver that she didn't get out of those cords alone, and I should be prepared to risk another fiver that it was John Cook who released her. Lord knows how he got there and then got away in the very nick of time—but that is my reading of the situation."

"And why did he tie her up and then let her go?" pursued the Sergeant.

"How did you know that he did tie her up?" asked his chief.

"But the cord, sir, and the handkerchief!"

"Circumstantial evidence, my dear Cunningham, is never entirely satisfactory," said Shelley, "and all the more so in a case like this, where there are all sorts of conflicting interests involved."

And with that Cunningham had perforce to be contented, for they were outside the offices of Mr. Bellingham.

"Do you think that we shall find him at his office as late as this?" asked Cunningham apprehensively. It was past six o'clock, and his query seemed reasonable.

"I am told," said Shelley, as they walked up the stairs, "that Mr. Bellingham has a habit of working rather later than most solicitors.

Whether that means that Mr. Bellingham does business which does not really lie within the province of a solicitor I don't know. But some day I shall make it my business to find out."

And Cunningham thought, as he glanced at Shelley's grimly-set face, that he would not like to be in the solicitor's shoes when that day arrived.

It seemed, at any rate, as if Shelley's information had been correct. There was a light in the solicitor's office, and Mr. Bellingham himself answered their knock.

"Mr. Shelley, this is a surprise," he said, motioning them to chairs, "I hope that you will forgive me a moment if I finish a conversation on the phone which your coming interrupted. I am sorry, but business is business, you know."

Shelley nodded, and Mr. Bellingham took up the receiver.

Sorry, sir," he said, after a moment, "but a good friend of mine, Mr. Shelley, has just arrived, and I am afraid that I must deal with him. Our talk would be likely to take some time, and I must ring you up later. Eh? Tomorrow morning suit you? Very well. Good-bye." And he rang off.

"That's that, then, Mr. Shelley," he said, turning to them with a pleasant smile, "and now what can I do for you?"

"I'm afraid that our errand is not a particularly pleasant one," said Shelley, feeling his way in his customary manner, and being, if truth were told, more than a little surprised to see a sudden look of fear in the other's eyes.

"Well, what is it, man? Get on with it," said Bellingham.

"It is just this, Mr. Bellingham," said Shelley, "when and where and how did you first make the acquaintance of Mr. John Cook?"

Bellingham drew a deep breath. Shelley could have sworn that the solicitor had been about to heave a very fervent sigh of relief.

Mastering himself, however, Bellingham merely smiled.

"I don't really know that that is a question that I can answer directly, Mr. Shelley," he said, "because, strictly speaking, I did not make his acquaintance. He made mine."

"I was not aware that there was much difference in the two cases," said Shelley, "come, Mr. Bellingham, how did you get to know this man? As you probably are aware, he has disappeared, and no one seems to know who he is."

"He is," said Mr. Bellingham," the founder, president and managing director of the National Anti-Speed Association, Limited."

"Well," smiled Shelley, "even the much-hated experts at Scotland Yard know that. What else can you tell me about him?"

"Very little, I fear," said Bellingham, "because I only made his acquaintance in the way of business. He came to me about six months ago, and wanted me to have a look at the prospectus of the association which he was just starting. He wanted to know if it was legal and in order."

"Do you specialise in that kind of work?" asked Shelley.

"Can't say that I do," answered the solicitor, "but he said that he wanted me to do the work for him. I advised him to go to some other solicitor more especially acquainted with company law and so on. But he said that he preferred that I should do the work."

"Was the thing all right?" It was, rather surprisingly, Cunningham who asked the question. He looked rather apprehensively at his chief, but Shelley nodded encouragingly.

"Quite all right," said the solicitor, "in fact, it looked almost as if it had been drawn up by a solicitor well versed in company law. The phraseology and so on was so exactly correct that I felt almost suspicious about it."

"Did you ask Mr. Cook to explain that fact?" asked Shelley.

"I did, and his explanation struck me as being a pretty lame one," admitted Bellingham.

"He said that he had done a good deal of investment, and that he had made such a study of company law that he found little difficulty in doing the thing as well as a solicitor would do."

"Then why come to a solicitor about it?"

"Exactly," said Mr. Bellingham, nodding his grey head portentously, "exactly. That was what I wondered myself. But it doesn't do to refuse business, you know, doesn't do at all. Besides, who could say that this Anti-Speed Association might not develop into a big thing—and then, as consulting solicitor to the firm, I might be doing well. I hope that you understand my position."

Shelley understood. He saw that no man of business would refuse work, even though it seemed to him that the client was perfectly capable of doing that work for himself.

"And that was the first time that you met Mr. Cook?" was Shelley's next question.

"The first time," Bellingham agreed.

"Did he give any references?" asked the Inspector.

"His bank: that was all," said Bellingham.

"The Chancery Lane Branch of Doidge's Bank. He had a deposit there of something approaching fifty thousand pounds. I know that, because he showed me his deposit book."

"Can you tell us anything that will throw light on his mysterious disappearance?" asked Shelley.

"I'm afraid that I cannot," said Bellingham, "in fact, mysterious is the only word that aptly describes it. He was a man, as far as I could judge, perfectly satisfied with life. He had plenty of money, and this Association of his was something to live for. He was an enthusiast on the subject, and the last man that I should have imagined would take his life or disappear wantonly in any way."

"Why do you think he may have committed suicide?" asked Shelley bluntly.

"I don't," answered the other, "but when a man vanishes like this, and doesn't leave a trace behind, you can't help wondering what has happened to him."

With that they had to be content. Bellingham could give them no more information, although he volunteered, courteously enough, to let Scotland Yard know if he came across any information which seemed likely to be of use.

He had, he said, certain papers in connection with the National Anti-Speed Association, and these might possibly contain some clue which would put him on the trail of the missing man. He did not think it likely, but he would look them through, and let them know the result later.

"And that," said Shelley, as they walked down Chancery Lane, "is that."

"And it's mighty little," added Cunningham.

"Mighty little!" exclaimed Shelley, "why, it's nothing at all! Do you know, all that Bellingham told us may be true: but if it's all lies, we shall be none the wiser. Hardly anything is confirmable; only a few details, like the name of his bank, which we could equally well have obtained from Miss Latimer."

"What's the next move, sir?" asked Cunningham.

"Since the hour is six o'clock or later," said Shelley (as a matter of fact, it was nearer seven), "and we have neither of us eaten since Lord knows when, the next move is towards a meal." And it was.

CHAPTER XII

HAPPENINGS IN BAYSWATER

A T the best of times Bayswater is not a very thrilling place: and that night Margery found it almost unbearably dull. She had gone through all sorts of exciting experiences and now, apparently, she was to settle down, calmly, to talk to Jean McKean or to read a novel.

Wanting company above all things, she went along to her friend's room for awhile.

But Jean seemed to have little to talk about, except clothes and film stars. Margery, like most girls of her age and time, was interested in dress: she also, on occasion, visited the cinema. But it seemed to her that chatter about Jean's new evening frock, or a comparison of Clark Gable and Herbert Marshall did not provide that touch of excitement which her mood demanded.

So, after half an hour's fruitless conversation with Jean, she returned to her own room, there to try to bury herself in a novel, the futile pages of which seemed to swim before her eyes. It was no good. She could not interest herself in anything. Before she could get back to the old routine of her life, some of the pressing problems of the present would have to be settled somehow. That was one of the drawbacks of living in an atmosphere of melodrama, she told herself, and then sighed heavily at the thought that she would have to wait for several hours before she returned to Fleet Street, and really faced up to the whole mad puzzle anew.

It was just as she had come to this decision that a timid knock came at her door.

"Come in," said Margery, and one of the servants entered.

"If you please, miss," she announced, "there's a gentleman downstairs asking for you. I showed him into the private drawing-room, and asked him to wait while I found if you were in."

"What is his name?" asked Margery, with some curiosity. Her male visitors were not many, and she could not make out who this could be. She did not think that John would take the almost incredible risk of coming here, and Shelley was, it would seem, almost the only other possibility.

"He wouldn't give his name, miss," said the maid, "but he said that if you would read this you'd understand what he was calling about." She handed Margery a sealed envelope, addressed, in a queer spidery hand to "Miss Margery Latimer."

Margery tore it open hurriedly, and, on reading what she saw inside, felt herself going pale beneath the servant's stony glare. This, the servant was no doubt thinking, was not the sort of thing that was expected to happen in a respectable boarding house. Margery was not worried about that, however: she was seriously perturbed at the contents of the note. Her heart had almost missed a beat when she read the letter. The thought that her beloved John was in danger was the only thing required to make her excitement bubble over.

For the note read: "If you wish to save J. C. from prison and perhaps worse, you will please see me. I have information which the police would be very glad to share, but I shall not let them know about it until I have seen you." The note was unsigned, and there was no clue to the identity of the writer.

"All right," said Margery, when at length she had gained control over herself, "I will see him, I suppose. The private drawing-room, you said?"

"Yes, miss," said the maid, "he's not exactly the sort of gentleman that Miss Walker would care to have in the public rooms of the house." Miss Walker, it should be mentioned, was the austere lady who managed the house and the "private drawing-room" was an invention of her own. It was a tiny little place—not much more than a box-room—but it enabled guests who wished for private interviews, and who did not care to receive their friends in a bed-sitting room which had a strong accent on the "bed," to meet conveniently.

When Margery entered this unique apartment she began to understand why the man was not considered quite suitable for admission to the public rooms of the house. He was not at all an unpleasant-looking man, but he had the word "servant" written all over him. That unpleasantly obsequious manner which somehow seems to mark off those who have been all their lives at the beck and call of others, was definitely to be seen. Otherwise, he was all right, from the neatly-brushed shoes on his feet to the cleanly-kept bowler hat which usually adorned his brown head and was now held in his hand.

"You wish to see me?" asked Margery, in her coldest tones.

"I regret to say, madam, that I do," he said, in the perfectly modulated voice of the well-trained servant.

"Well, I'm here," said Margery, "and will you please say whatever you have to say as quickly as possible?"

"Certainly, madam," he said, motioning her to a chair.

"I prefer to stand, thank you," said Margery, but he waved imperiously again, and she sat down.

"My story may take some little time," he said, "and I think that you will be pleased to have something to rest upon by the time that I have finished."

"Go on," was the only comment Margery had to offer.

"It happens, madam," he said, "to have come to my knowledge that you are—shall we say well acquainted?—with Mr. John Cook of pious memory." Margery started at the phrase. It seemed to suggest that John was dead. But her visitor's next words belied that. "I am sure," he went on, "that you do not wish to see Mr. Cook in prison, or even in danger of the gallows. Hanging is not a pleasant death, Miss Latimer."

"Will you please get to the point, and not beat about the bush in this manner?" Margery interrupted.

"Certainly, madam," he said, "nothing will please me more. I happen to know, then, that Mr. John Cook was in the street outside this house on the night of the murder of Sir Henry

Henshaw. Ah, I see you know that as well." For Margery, in spite of her attempt at self-control, had been unable to repress the violent start at this sudden revelation of what she had always conceived to be a secret of her own.

"In any case," went on her visitor, "this is not all the information which I have at my disposal. I also know that at the time that Lord Chaney was killed on the stairs of Mr. Bellingham's office in Chancery Lane Mr. Cook was, to put it mildly, within a few hundred yards of the spot."

"The police know that already," said Margery.

"Oh, yes, but do they know," asked the stranger, "that Mr. Cook had emerged from the door less than two minutes when Mr. Bellingham discovered Lord Chaney's body? But in spite of the fact that the police know something of the facts which I have given you already, there remains what is perhaps the most important fact of all. I know that Mr. Cook was in Slough High Street within a few minutes of the death of Mr. Victor Dunn. I also know that Mr. Cook has or had in his possession several daggers of the kind used to stab the three unfortunate speed-merchants (if I may be permitted to describe the deceased gentlemen by what is a piece of bad journalese). And what do you think of that information, Miss Latimer?"

"Can you prove it?" That was all that concerned Margery. She was vitally concerned that John should not be betrayed to the police. Rather than that she would kill this man with her own hands!

"I have witnesses in each instance," he replied calmly, "and, in case you should be meditating any violence against my person, I would mention that all this information has been placed in a vault of the Chancery Lane Safe Deposit, addressed to Scotland Yard. In the event of my death or disappearance, that will be opened and sent off. So you will gain nothing by disposing of me, my dear young lady!"

"What do you want?" asked Margery.

He smiled evilly at her, revealing a set of perfect teeth as he did so, but yet showing some kind of leering unpleasantness in his expression.

"What is it that we all want in these bad times?" he said. "Money, of course, Miss Latimer, money! That's what I want."

"How much?" Margery managed to utter the words, although her heart was lead.

"Five thousand pounds would, I think, be ample," said he.

"Five thousand pounds! Where do you think that I can lay hands on such a sum?" exclaimed Margery, "it's quite an impossible sum for me."

"For you, yes," he replied, "but for the National Anti-Speed Association, no. I am aware that you have Mr. Cook's written authority to write cheques in his absence. And the sum on deposit in the name of the Association is far in excess of the puny amount which I am asking for."

"Blackmail can't be a very pleasant way of earning a living, can it?" asked Margery deliberately.

"And don't think, young lady, that you will make things any better by being insulting," he said, his face livid with anger, "I am quite capable of asking for more money if you don't do as I ask."

"So I should imagine," said Margery, cool and even outwardly, although inside her heart she was feeling the weight of despair. If this man knew as much about Cook as he said, how could he ever be got rid of? He would drain the Association dry of money, and then, if Cook came back, how would she account for it?

"You don't want it immediately, I suppose," she went on, "because if you do, I am afraid that you will be sadly disappointed. I couldn't draw out five thousand pounds in a lump sum without attracting too much comment. Besides, I'm not at all sure that the bank would let me have it without some sort of explanation."

"Very well," he said, "I'll give you two days to think it over, and then I will ring you up to learn of your decision. I shall want at least two thousand within a week, however, or else the police will know!"

He got up, bowed to her ironically, and was gone. For a moment Margery sat still, almost broken with worry, but then, suddenly making her decision, she hurried to her room, jammed a hat on her head, grasped a mackintosh and hurried out. Here was a possibility of action at last! It was what she wanted!

Just at the end of the street she saw her man. He was emerging into Queen's Road, and she saw him hurry towards the Underground Station. He took a District train, and Margery, who had run down the stairs, breathlessly, after him, managed to seat herself in the next carriage, where she could watch the exit from the carriage which the blackmailer occupied.

At Paddington, the next station, he got out, and walked in a leisurely manner up to the Great Western Station. Margery followed him as cautiously as she knew how, having one or two moments of acute anxiety as he looked around him like one wondering if he were followed. He did not see her, however, and she blessed the lucky chance which placed a very fat old man between them as they waited in the queue opposite the booking office.

He asked for a single to Slough, and Margery booked a return to the same place, not bothering any longer to keep very close to her quarry.

It would be as well, she thought, to give him a fairly long lead, although she was fully resolved to travel by the same train as her visitor, and, if possible, to track him to his lair.

It proved surprisingly simple, as it happened, for he sauntered down the platform, and got into the first reasonably empty compartment which offered itself. Margery, who had taken the precaution of buying a paper behind which she could hide, followed suit, getting into a compartment a little further along the same coach.

That short journey to Slough kept her on tenterhooks. All the time she was wondering if her actions would have any tangible result. She had followed the blackmailer in this way, acting purely on impulse. And she wondered, even now, what she hoped to get out of it. It was possible, of course, that he was in some way involved in the crimes himself. He certainly had known a lot about the circumstances surrounding them. And there had been cases before when a criminal had blackmailed some perfectly innocent person. She no longer had to keep telling herself that John was innocent: since that wonderful moment when he had released her from her bonds she had never had more than momentary doubts on the matter, and now even those were no more. He was innocent, she felt sure, and it was up to her to prove his innocence. This exploit of hers gave her a chance to do something towards that end, and she felt almost grateful towards the blackmailer when she thought of her helpless feelings of such a short time before.

Slough arrived at last, however, and Margery, looking carefully out of the window, saw her man walking slowly along the platform towards the exit. Quickly she descended to the platform and was soon following in his wake. He emerged from the station and made his way towards the High Street, Margery still keeping close on his heels. For one dreadful moment she thought that he had seen her. He paused and looked around him, but she managed to get into a shop doorway before he looked her way.

Then, when she was beginning to think that he was making towards his home, he walked into a garage. It was just off the High Street, and was one of those huge concrete, and corrugated iron erections which the post-war expansion produced in such numbers all along the Great West Road.

Margery waited at the other side of the road, and looked at the building opposite.

He seemed to be taking a long time there, for it was some minutes before Margery could make up her mind what was happening. The minutes extended into a quarter of an hour, then into half an hour, until at last Margery took her courage into both hands, and decided to walk into the place and pursue, as she put it in her mind, the lion into his den.

"Yes, madam," said a grimy garage attendant, as she entered, "what can we do for you?"

"I was passing here just now," she said, "and I thought I saw a friend of mine come in here. A Mr. Jones." And she described the man as minutely as she could. "I thought," she added, "that he might still be here, or, if not, that you might be able to give me his address. I've lost touch with him for years, but I heard that he was living in Slough."

"I think I know the gentleman you mean, madam," said the garage attendant, "although I don't know his name. He was. only enquiring about a car he thought of buying. He didn't give us his name and address, so I'm afraid that I can't help you."

Again Margery felt annoyed with herself.

Had she let the man slip through her fingers somehow?

"Did you see which way he went?" she asked.

"I'm afraid I didn't," said the man, "but he went out through our side-entrance. Out this way, you see."

He led the way to a small door, and let her out into a small side street. It was obvious that the man had thought himself followed—or else that he took this course as a means of making sure that he should not be seen. In any case, it seemed that he was lost to her for the time.

"Thank you so much," she said smiling at the garage man, and handing him a half-crown. Then she felt almost like weeping as he closed the door behind her. It was certainly bad luck that the blackmailer had managed to elude her in this way.

And then she caught a glimpse of the name of the street on a metal plate in the wall above her head.

"Albert Road, leading to Albert Square," it said. Margery racked her brains. Where had she heard of Albert Square before? And then, quite suddenly, remembrance came to her. It was the address of Victor Dunn who had been murdered! And now she was led to the very spot by a man who said that he knew all about the crime! What did it all mean? It did not seem to take her much further forward in her search for proofs of John Cook's innocence, but she could not help feeling a queer sensation of elation as she made her way back to the station, *en route* for Paddington once more.

CHAPTER XIII

WHO IS THE STRANGER?

MARGERY went to work the next morning with a lighter heart. It was quite impossible to explain, for it seemed as if the very fact of the existence of the stranger was a menace to the freedom and even the life of John Cook. But still the feeling of satisfaction was there. Next time, she told herself, she would really find out who he was and where he lived—and then put Scotland Yard on his track.

But—she wondered—would it not be better to tell the detective about the existence of this stranger now? She had no longer any fear that he might be able to imperil John's safety. That feeling had left her, never to return. Impetuous as ever, she rang up the Yard and asked for Shelley. In a moment he was at the phone, and promised to come straight over immediately.

"Now, Miss Latimer," he was saying a few minutes later, "what is it that you have to say? You haven't remembered something about Mr. Cook, I suppose? Something that will put us on the track of that elusive personality?" The pleasant smile with which he uttered these words took away the unfortunate air of sarcasm which the mere words suggested.

"Nothing like that, Mr. Shelley," Margery answered, "and there is not likely to be anything like that for you, at any rate for some time to come. But what I've got to tell you is more important than information which will put you on the track of Mr. Cook. It is information which will put you on the track of the murderer!"

A sudden intake of breath, so sharp as to be almost a whistle, was the only indication that Shelley gave of his very real surprise at hearing these words.

"Well," he said, "go on."

"You don't seem very much surprised, Mr. Shelley," said

Margery, in aggrieved tones, "but then I suppose that it would take a lot to surprise the mystery man of Scotland Yard."

He smiled again. "I can tell you one thing, Miss Latimer," he said, "I shall be very considerably surprised if your information is really as important as you seem to think it."

"Well," said Margery, "here it is." And she told him the whole story of the previous evening's work, as it has already been narrated in the last chapter of this history. He sat there opposite her, looking straight at her face, gazing unblinkingly at her until the tale was told. The fact that he made no interruptions, but merely permitted her to speak for nearly ten minutes, was sufficient indication of his interest.

"Well done!" he exclaimed when she had finished, "I don't think that one of my men could have told that story better than you have, Miss Latimer."

"But don't you believe it?" asked Margery, in dismay.

"Of course I believe it," he returned, "and I admire your courage in telling what you feel must at present seem to support the case against Mr. Cook. By the way," he added in his most deliberately casual tones, "you are in love with our friend Cook, aren't you?"

Margery felt the blush creeping over her face. It was ridiculous, she told herself, that she should show such a Victorian sign of emotion, but she could not help herself.

"I—er—I think I am," she admitted at length.

"Then," he said, "I should ask you, Miss Latimer, to remember that I am compelled to do my duty, no matter who it may implicate. All the same, I shall remember that you have told me this story, even though it may seem, on the surface, to hurt the man whom you love."

Margery felt, once again, that leaden grip at her heart as he spoke. Did he mean that John was in some way involved in this web of mystery? Did he mean that he was building up a case against the man she loved? For a moment she felt like cursing the impulse which had led her to share her information with the man from Scotland Yard. But then she took courage again. Had she not convinced herself that John was entirely innocent of this terrible crime? Had she not made up her mind that she would find the real culprit? And was not the best policy to tell the police all the truth always? Painfully obvious it was to her that she had not herself lived up to this dictum, but she registered a mental vow that in future she would do so.

"Now," said Shelley, suddenly recalling her thoughts back to the present moment, "I wonder if you will answer a question or two about this man."

Margery nodded. "Help the police," she told herself, "and they will get their man in the end!"

"First of all, a complete description of him," said the detective.

She thought for a moment, and then replied. "Five feet eight or nine in height," she said, "brown curly hair, brown eyes, good teeth, clean-shaven. Navy blue suit, fawn mackintosh, bowler hat, black shoes. Age—oh, about thirty-five or six, I should think."

"Excellent so far," commented Shelley, "and now—any special peculiarities of manner?"

"He struck me," said Margery, "as being a superior servant of some kind. Butler or footman perhaps—he might even be a waiter in a good-class restaurant."

"That," said Shelley, "is exactly what I think he is. Not a waiter, but a butler, I mean."

Margery was amazed. "Do you know who he is?" she asked.

"I'm fairly sure about it," said Shelley, "and if you will come along to Slough with me this afternoon I think that you will be able to help me to arrest the gentleman."

"Who is it?" asked Margery.

"I don't think that I should tell you that," answered Shelley cautiously, "it might prejudice your identification this afternoon. You see, I think that he is in some way involved in the murder, and this blackmail charge of yours will give us a reason for holding him in custody whilst the other case is completed."

And there he left the problem at the moment.

Margery could not persuade him to say any more. He assured her that in a few hours the whole business—at any rate as far as the mysterious stranger was concerned—would be solved.

That afternoon she travelled down to Slough once more, having shut up the office and given Adolphus yet another afternoon off, much to that youth's surprise and pleasure. This time, however, Margery was not in a train, but in one of the special fast cars attached to Scotland Yard's flying squad.

In Slough they speeded along the High Street, and she nudged the detective's arm as they came opposite the side street a few yards down which stood the garage in which the stranger had gone the night before.

"I know," he said, "but we're going another way. Don't want to frighten our bird, you know."

Soon they went down another side street, and came out into a wide and spacious square which was clearly one of the few remaining relics of the day when Slough was a small and compact Victorian country town.

"Now you are to remain here," said Shelley to her when the car stopped, "I shall come out of that house presently, with a man who will, I think, be the man we want. If I am correct in my suspicion, all that you have to do is to say 'Yes' as I come opposite the car with him. I shall then arrest him, and we shall take him back to town with us. If I'm wrong (but I don't think that I am) we shall have to begin all over again."

He walked over to one of the big houses of the square, and Margery, craning her neck in an effort to see, made out the number "6" on the gate. It was someone connected with Mr. Dunn's house, then! She wondered who it could be.

But Shelley was gone a very long time. To Margery,

impatiently waiting there in the car, it seemed much longer than it was. Actually, a quarter of an hour had elapsed before he returned to her, and he came alone.

"Has the bird flown then?" she whispered eagerly, as he approached.

He shook his head wearily. "Not exactly," he said, "but I'm afraid that we shan't get much information out of him. I wonder if you can stand a shock, Miss Latimer?"

"Of course I can," she said, "what's the trouble?"

"The trouble is," he said soberly, "that your visitor of last night, the man whom you tracked back here, is dead!"

"Dead!" Margery uttered the word between tightly-drawn lips. Her face had suddenly paled beneath this shock.

"Yes," answered the detective, "murdered. Stabbed with the same kind of knife as those which were used in the previous murders!"

Margery was amazed at this new crime, and she saw immediately how it would appear to the detective's mind. The man had threatened to go to the police with information about John Cook, and he was murdered almost immediately. It would certainly appear, from the point of view of the police, as if John Cook was the murderer, and had committed yet another crime in a vain effort to destroy the evidence against him.

"What are you going to do?" she asked Shelley.

"The Slough police have the matter in hand," he replied, "But the case will be handed over to Scotland Yard as soon as I can communicate with headquarters. It is quite certainly connected with the earlier crimes." He spoke gently, as if he were sorry for her, as no doubt he was.

"Do you want me any more?" she asked faintly. The case against Cook seemed to grow stronger with every moment.

"Well," he said, "if you could manage to brace yourself against the shock, I should like you to identify the body. He's not nasty to look at," he added, as if that would make any difference to the unpleasantness of the case, "he's been nicely tidied up by the local police surgeon, who's been examining him."

Margery nodded again. "All right," she said, "I'll do it, Mr. Shelley."

"Come in, then," he said, taking her arm, and leading her over to the door, where they were received by a white-faced and trembling maid.

They walked slowly up the stairs and into a bedroom at the back of the house. Subconsciously she took in the appearance of the place. It would have been a pleasant enough room under normal circumstances, with its bright wallpaper, its modern furniture and the shelf of books, with brilliantly coloured "jackets" which hung on the wall opposite her.

At the moment, however, all this was out of place in the circumstances. Her eyes were attracted inevitably to the still form on the bed. The man was laid out peacefully enough, but the copious stains of blood on the bedclothes told their own story.

Only one glance at his face was necessary.

"That's the man," she told Shelley.

"Very well," he said, and led her gently from the room.

"When," she faltered, as they walked down the stairs, "when was he . . . when did it . . .?"

"It happened at ten o'clock last night," he said, "or about that time. Anyhow, that is the verdict of the police surgeon."

"Is anything known about it?" she asked, "I mean, have the police any clue?"

"Nothing up to the moment," he answered, "and you may be sure that I shall let you know as soon as anything is found out. about it. In the meantime, my job is to see you safely home. I have the dead man's fingerprints, also, to take to the Yard for comparison with our files. I'll drop you on the way."

He did not speak a word on the way back to Bayswater, and as they passed down the Queen's Road he merely pointed down the side-road in which she lived, raising his eyebrows questioningly meanwhile.

Margery nodded, and he uttered a curt word of command into the speaking tube which communicated with the driver.

"Thank you," she said to him, and he handed her out of the car with as little emotion as if she had been a "drunk and disorderly" whom he was delivering at the nearest police station.

Once in the house, Margery made her way straight to her room. Then, just as she was taking her hat off, and sinking down wearily on the bed, she remembered that she had omitted to ask Shelley for what was a vital piece of information.

Who was the stranger? It seemed to her essential that she should know. Shelley would soon be at the Yard, however, and she could ring him up then.

Giving him ten minutes she went to the phone in the hall, and asked for Scotland Yard. She would, she thought, get through more quickly if she asked for it in that way than if she dialled the number in the usual manner.

"Inspector Shelley, please," she said briskly, and the curt official at the other end put her through to Shelley's office without delay.

"I'm sorry to worry you so soon, Mr. Shelley," she said, when she had heard his familiar voice at the other end of the wire, "but I forgot to ask you an important question."

"Yes," he said, "what is it that you want to know, Miss Latimer. Quick, please, if you don't mind. I'm very busy."

"Who was my visitor last night?" she asked, "Who is the man who died?"

"His real name I don't know yet," said Shelley, "but he has been on our files here for a long time. We identified him by those finger-prints I told you about. The report from the finger-print department came through just as you phoned."

"He was a criminal?" she asked.

"Yes," he said, "he was known in criminal circles as Bertie

the Butler. Made a speciality of getting jobs as a butler or some servant's post, in households where there were valuable secrets to be picked up. Then he would 'put on the black,' as the crooks say."

"Blackmailer!" she murmured the word comprehendingly, and then "But what was he doing in Mr. Dunn's house?" she asked.

"I was a fool not to have spotted him before," said Shelley, "the latest name he was going under was Williamson. He was the butler in the house of the late Mr. Dunn!"

CHAPTER XIV

WHAT DOES MR. BELLINGHAM KNOW?

M ARGERY slept badly that night, and her slumbers were disturbed by horrible dreams. At one moment she would be in a dark cavern, knowing that at the other end was a mysterious assassin with a knife, and then, after a sudden, shuddering awakening, she would fall asleep again, only to see John Cook's lifeless body swinging from the gibbet. It was the most disturbed night that she ever remembered spending.

The result, as might have been expected, was that she awoke the next morning with a splitting headache, ate no breakfast, and felt like nothing on earth on her arrival at the office.

She was wondering what she should do to while away the time. For work was almost at a standstill. Cook had been the initiator of all the schemes which the Anti-Speed Association had been carrying out, and now that his guiding hand was gone, there seemed practically nothing to be done. Margery felt that she owed it to John to turn up each morning as if nothing were altered, but she felt, sometimes, as if he would never come back, and she would never be happy again.

But she never let Adolphus see that this feeling of despondency was gradually gaining a hold on her. To the little office-boy she was always bright and cheerful, always the same Miss Latimer, with a happy smile for all the world, that he had grown, boy-like, to admire.

On this morning, however, what with the terrible facts of the murder of Williamson to face, and the additional burden of her headache, Margery was hard put to it to keep a cheerful countenance when Adolphus was present, and when he left her at midday to go and get his lunch, she locked the outer door, and let herself relax. She leant her head on her arms and sobbed as if her heart would break. Somehow the flow of tears seemed to bring relief to her tired spirit.

Suddenly she sat up with a start. Surely that was a knock at the outer door? Yes, there it was again! Margery hurriedly dried her eyes, and hastily applied the ever-necessary powder to hide the ravages of grief. Then, when a glance at the little mirror in her handbag seemed to her sufficiently reassuring, she went to the door.

She was surprised to see an old friend. There at the door, his hat in his hand, his lithe, short figure looking like a youth's, until one caught sight of the grey head and the military moustache, was Mr. Bellingham!

"Why, Mr. Bellingham," exclaimed Margery, "this is a real surprise. I haven't seen you for ages—not since I came here to work, I think."

"No, my dear," he said, "nor I you, except for an occasional glimpse of you when you passed up Chancery Lane."

"Come in and sit down," said Margery, "I have very little work to do at the moment. Everything has gone wrong, you know, since Mr. Cook has disappeared. At any rate, there doesn't seem to be much to do."

"I'm afraid that the job I gave you—or rather got for you," said Mr. Bellingham, correcting himself with an air of confusion, "was not as good as I had hoped. However, we must just hope for the best, and expect that Mr. Cook will turn up again before very long."

"Oh, I expect he will," replied Margery, expressing a conviction which, in her present mood, she was far from feeling, "but I suppose that in the meantime I must just carry on as best I can. That's what I'm trying to do, anyhow."

"Good girl," said Mr. Bellingham, with a touch of that air of patronage which he had always shown towards her, ever since she could remember, "good girl. But I didn't come here to talk about that. What I wanted to say was this: I don't think that we are seeing enough of one another nowadays. After all, I was your guardian for goodness knows how many years."

"Now, Mr. Bellingham," said Margery playfully, "don't try to make me older than I am. I shall become an old maid soon enough as it is, without those suggestions of years and years which you seem to be inclined to make."

He chuckled. It was an old man's laugh, which belied the comparative youthfulness of his form and bearing.

"Yes, my dear," he said, "you are quite right. You are not so old as all that. But what am I saying? I don't seem able to stick to the point today. What I really called in here for was to ask you if you would have dinner with me tonight. Just take pity on a lonely old man, you know, and share a frugal meal."

Margery, whose turn it now was to laugh, knew those frugal meals of his. It would, she had no doubt, be the best that could be had at the Savoy or the National Liberal Club, or some equally formidable place (to her) could supply.

"I should be delighted, Mr. Bellingham," she said, "but why this sudden desire for my company?"

"To tell you the truth, Margery," he said, "there is something quite important which I want to discuss with you. It is not," he added, with his customary cautiousness of diction, "unconnected with the disappearance of Mr. Cook. And I think that you are the person to whom I should talk about it."

Margery started. What did her old guardian and employer know about John Cook? She remembered that Shelley had once mentioned the possibility of getting some information from Mr. Bellingham, but she did not remember that he had pursued the idea further than a mere suggestion.

"It is all very mysterious, Mr. Bellingham," she said.

"And I am afraid that it must so remain, my dear," he said, "until tonight. I cannot talk at any length now, as you may have someone coming in at any moment, and if we have a private room somewhere this evening all will be well. Then we shall be able to talk at length and get the whole thing settled once and for all."

"When and where shall I meet you, then?" she asked.

He hesitated before replying. "I will call for you at your lodging," he said, "and we can go straight to the Savoy. I can get a small private dining-room there whenever I want it, I know. Shall we say half-past seven tonight?"

"All right," Margery agreed, and there the matter was left for the time being.

It is to be feared that she did not concentrate very much on what little work there was to do that afternoon. The mysterious hints about John Cook which Mr. Bellingham had persisted in throwing out worried her. What had he meant to imply? That was the problem which he had set her, and lacking all the necessary data, she was unable to solve it that afternoon, although she thought all around the question for hours that seemed to be endless.

At last, however, it was time to go home, and, dressing in her newest evening frock and placing a rose, which she had bought, on her shoulder, she thought that she was sufficiently respectable to face the critical eyes of the frequenters of the Savoy.

Mr. Bellingham was in good time. His cab called for her at precisely twenty-five minutes past seven, and Mr. Bellingham, in immaculate evening dress, greeted her appearance with delight.

"Wherever do you manage to get these delightful clothes, my dear?" he asked, gazing at the cloak which she had thrown over her dress.

"I buy them, of course, Mr. Bellingham," she said, "you forget that I am no longer a penniless wage-slave, working myself to death in a grumpy old solicitor's office. I am now a lady secretary (or so the agencies describe it), earning five hundred a year. I can afford lovely clothes."

He acknowledged the thrust with a chuckle, and changed the subject.

"I hope that the Savoy will be all right?" he said anxiously, "there is nowhere else that you would rather go, is there?"

"I don't mind where we go," answered Margery, "I'd go to the Hotel Cecil if it weren't pulled down."

"That's all right, then," he said, with a contented sigh, and settled back in his seat with the air of one who has done his duty nobly.

But Margery felt that there was some unusual constraint about his manner, as if he were meditating the wisdom of this interview. He watched her covertly from beneath his half-closed eyelids. From an occasional sidelong glance that she managed to cast at him surreptitiously she was aware of that. He seemed to be studying her carefully, as if not quite sure of his ground.

He did not, however, say another word until after their arrival in the Strand, and as they drove up that famous thoroughfare, he asked if there were anything in particular which she would wish to have included in the dinner that night.

"I always thought, Mr. Bellingham," said Margery, who felt, somehow, in a roguish mood, "that it was the host's privilege to select the dishes which he should place before his guest."

"Agreed, my dear," he said, "but as we are nothing so formal as host and guest, but just two old friends having dinner together, I thought that you might care to have a hand in the choosing of the meal."

"No thank you," said she, "I am well content to leave it to you."

And so to him it was left. A very pleasant meal it turned out to be, too, although its enjoyment for Margery was spoilt by a thought of what was coming after. Mr. Bellingham was one of the old-fashioned folk who think that serious conversation during meals should be taboo. Consequently he insisted that they should talk only of flippant, foolish things while the dinner was being eaten, and Margery was hard put to it to keep her end up at this kind of conversation.

At last, however, the meal was over. As Mr. Bellingham pushed back his chair a little from the table with a sigh of pleasure, and handed her his cigarette case, Margery thought that the serious part of the evening's business had really begun. They were alone in the room, for Mr. Bellingham had been true to his word, and had managed to get a private dining-room.

When they had got their cigarettes properly going, he plunged at once into the middle of the discussion.

"Do you think," he began, "that the police are handling this business properly?"

"What business?" asked Margery.

"Why the business of these dreadful murders," he said, "and the disappearance of poor Cook. It appears to me as if there were some serious mismanagement somewhere."

"I'm afraid that I don't quite understand you, Mr. Bellingham," said Margery, "where do you think that there has been mismanagement?"

"It's goodness knows how many weeks since the first murder occurred," he explained, "you know, that poor fellow who was killed in Bayswater. And then there were two more. Then Cook disappeared and now we have the fourth murder."

"You really think that they are connected—all these crimes, I mean?" asked Margery.

"Well, my dear Margery," he expostulated, "could it be possible that they are not? Four murders, three of them of prominent men in the motor-racing world, and the fourth of a servant of one of those men. The disappearance of a man who is working for the elimination of speed from our modern life. Isn't the connection obvious?"

"You mean that you think John Cook guilty of those atrocious crimes?" she asked.

"I'm very much afraid that he is," said Mr. Bellingham.

"Well, I'm perfectly certain that he isn't!" said Margery. "And that's that!"

"What evidence have you for that remarkable statement?" asked Mr. Bellingham, and Margery noticed that his hand was trembling so that the ash fell off the end of his cigarette. Suppressed excitement, she supposed. Or was it merely old age?

"I've no material evidence at all," she was compelled to admit, "but I happen to know John Cook better than anyone else does, and I know that he doesn't know anything about it."

"He knows something about it all right," said Mr. Bellingham, with another chuckle, "but whether he is the murderer or not I must admit that there is a certain amount of doubt. Of course, the police would arrest him for it if they could lay hands on him—but the police, as I suggested just now, are not know-alls."

"But I tell you, he is innocent of anything criminal," Margery persisted.

"What the novelists are pleased to call feminine intuition, I suppose," said Mr. Bellingham, and Margery flushed at the sneer which he was unable altogether to eliminate from his voice.

"If you prefer to call it that—yes," said Margery, "but my term for it is knowledge of character. Psychological knowledge, if you like."

"Ah, you modern people!" Mr. Bellingham held up an admonishing hand. "Freud and all the others have gone to your heads! You think that psychology explains everything. It doesn't, you know. Not quite everything, anyhow."

All this talk—sometimes serious and sometimes bantering—was leaving Margery in a complete fog. That there was something behind it all, she knew. But what was Mr. Bellingham's object in asking for this interview? What was he really driving at?

"Was this all that you wanted to say, Mr. Bellingham?" she asked, looking at her watch in a manner which left no doubt of her meaning, "because, if so, I think that we might as well consider the conversation at an end. If your only reason for asking me here was to cast aspersions on the character of

Mr. Cook, there is nothing to be gained by going on with the interview. You think he is guilty. I *know* that he is innocent. And that is really all that there is to be said about the matter."

Her haughtiness of demeanour seemed to strike a sudden chill in Bellingham's heart. "No, no!" he said, grasping her arm so firmly that she gave a little gasp of pain, "you must not go yet! It's my own fault, for wandering off the point, you know. Most reprehensible trait in a solicitor." And he smiled weakly.

"Well, then, please Mr. Bellingham," she said, "will you cease to wander off the point and get on to it quickly. I have no desire to spend the whole evening discussing whether my knowledge of John Cook's character is of more value than your supposed evidence."

"What I really wanted to suggest, then, my dear," he said quickly, "was that we should put some private detective on John Cook's trail. It is for you that I am thinking. After all, you are the one that will lose most through being associated with a mystery of this kind."

"Of course, that might be so," said Margery, "but it may surprise you to know, Mr. Bellingham, that I have already had five offers of matrimony, from gentlemen quite unknown to me, since I became—shall we say notorious?—in connection with this case."

"You do surprise me!" he exclaimed. "But that is only one example of the kind of thing that I wish you to be protected from. Don't you see, my dear, that we must try to solve this problem, and until we do it, you will get all kinds of unnecessary and unpleasant publicity?"

"Do you really think," asked Margery, in amazement, "that one of these wretched little private detective agencies, whose main reason for existence is to shadow people in divorce cases, will be able to find John Cook for us?"

"There is one of them," he said, "which is far superior to the kind of work which you mention. Have you ever heard of Washington's?"

"Can't say I have," said Margery, "what is it?"

"It is," he told her, "the only really high-class detective agency in the British Isles. George Washington, the man at the head of it, he calls himself. He does that, so it is said, because then the public will know that he is out to find the truth. There is no question of hiding up what is found if you give Washington's the job. When there is anything against the law found out, they make it public, every word of it. That is a clause in the agreement which all their prospective clients have to sign."

"Do you know this George Washington?" asked Margery.

"No one knows him," answered Mr. Bellingham, "he keeps in the background always. One only sees a subordinate when one visits the office. No one, outside the office, knows if George Washington exists, even. He may be just a name to hide the fact that the firm has no real head—just a committee."

"How did you know all this then?"

Mr. Bellingham looked as if he were trying to be very clever. "That, my dear, is my secret," he said, "but I can tell you that it is the absolute truth. We can be sure that if John Cook is innocent, Washington's will do their best to establish that fact. If he is guilty, then that will be made public. If you are sure that your intuition is telling you the truth, then you will support me in this."

"All right," said Margery, "I will agree. But remember, Mr. Bellingham, whatever this Washington agency finds out, nothing will convince me that John is guilty."

It was the first time that she had used merely the Christian name in speaking to Mr. Bellingham of John Cook, and Margery was very conscious that he looked at her curiously as she did so.

It was as they were saying good-bye on the step of the taxi outside her Bayswater home, however, that Margery caught in Mr. Bellingham's face an expression which really amazed her.

"I hope my dear," he had said, "that if it turns out that this Washington chap does prove John Cook guilty, that you won't be too astonished. I hope that if he's dead, even, which is quite possible, that you won't be too hurt."

"I know he's not dead, anyhow," she said reassuringly, "and for that I can give you evidence."

"What's this evidence, then?" he asked.

"Why, the fact that I was speaking to him only two days ago," said Margery.

And it was at that moment that she caught the look in Bellingham's face, the look which surprised her more than anything else which she had observed during that very surprising evening. For, if her judgment was not very wrong, for one fleeting moment Mr. Bellingham's face was twisted out of its usual pleasant shape. And the expression which, for the moment, it bore, was fear—sheer agonising fear! Then he had jumped into the taxi, and was gone, whilst Margery, her thoughts too involved for words, was walking slowly up the steps to the house.

CHAPTER XV

"GEORGE WASHINGTON"

"GEORGE WASHINGTON, LTD." was the only inscription on the doorpost. Margery looked at it, a smile on her face, and her mind in utter confusion. Mr. Bellingham had insisted in dragging her off to this ridiculous place, and she was not at all sure she liked the idea. However, now that they were here, she might as well put a bright face on it, she thought.

Petty France was the name of the street, and a most extraordinary name Margery thought it. As a matter of fact, it is a name with an honoured history, ever since John Milton had his lodging there, but this Margery did not know.

When they got off the train at St. James's Park Underground Station, Margery was prepared for anything. "George Washington, Ltd., Petty France, S.W.1," was all the information which the telephone directory had vouchsafed her, and that was really nothing at all.

As she stood with Mr. Bellingham, irresolute, outside the tall, impressive-looking building which the great detective agency inhabited, she felt a sudden thrill of expectancy pass over her. Perhaps, after all, this man "George Washington," whoever he was, might help her to find John Cook at last! If so, it would be worth going through anything to get him. In recent hours, she had found herself wanting more and more to hear that pleasant voice, see that pleasant face smiling down at her. And (although she hardly dared to admit it, even to herself), she was beginning to fear that he was gone beyond recall.

"Come along, my dear," said Mr. Bellingham impatiently, "can't stay dreaming outside the place all day, you know. We must get on with the job. John Cook must be found, if it is at all possible, and these people are the people to do it."

So they went inside the main door of the building. There was not a soul in sight, and they looked around them as if they half-expected someone to materialise, with startling suddenness, from behind the door.

A lift was standing at the end of the corridor, its gates open invitingly.

"Let's see," said Margery, "if there's a liftman about."

As they approached, however, they saw that the door was open, not because a liftman was there, but because it was one of those automatic lifts which are operated by the user, without the assistance of any official. At any rate, that was what Margery decided must be the explanation, for no attendant was in sight, and a notice on the lift-gates read: "Please step in."

"Oh dear, oh dear," said Mr. Bellingham, "I never did like those lifts which one has to work oneself. They are apt to go wrong and stick between floors."

He overcame his dislike, however, and soon followed Margery into the lift. No sooner were they there than, without warning, the gates of the lift slammed to behind them, and the lift itself began to ascend.

"You really shouldn't have slammed those gates so loudly, my dear Margery," said Mr. Bellingham, "my nerves are not what they used to be, and I think that you might remember the fact."

"But I didn't slam the gates," said Margery, "I was looking for the button to press, the button that makes the lift move, I mean, and I thought that you had shut the gates."

"They must be automatic gates, then," said Mr. Bellingham, satisfied, "and that accounts for the dreadful noise that they made."

The lift stopped suddenly, and the gates opened with another clang that made Mr. Bellingham wince. Just opposite the gates of the lift there was a door, which bore, in white paint, the words, "George Washington, Ltd.," and, as they emerged on to the landing, this door opened before them, and they were enabled to see a large notice on the opposite wall, which read

"Please come in." No sooner had they complied with this request than the door shut behind them.

"All this tomfoolery about automatic doors and things," said Mr. Bellingham, "makes me sick! Trying to impress people, that's all they're doing."

"Well, it has the merit of being original, anyhow," said Margery, trying hard not to let a tremor creep into her voice. To tell truth, she found the impersonal attitude of this place more than a little frightening.

"Original bunkum!" retorted Mr. Bellingham, "their methods strike me as being more like an Egyptian fortune-teller's than a modern detective agency."

"Can I do anything to assist your predicament?" asked a voice behind them, soft, but insistent, and Margery nearly jumped out of her shoes. She could have sworn that there was only one door in the room, the door by which they had entered, and now, on turning round, she perceived another opening in the wall behind her. Standing in this opening, gazing at them with a benign stare, was an unmistakable Egyptian. The high cheek-bones and the well-cut suit did not blend together. The clothes were modern, she told herself, but the eyes were ancient—the eyes of Ancient Egypt itself.

"Who are you?" snapped Mr. Bellingham at the newcomer.

"I have the honour to represent George Washington," he purred at them. His voice was soft and gentle, but one had, somehow, the impression that it could, when necessary, be stern and forbidding.

"Then take us to your principal at once!" said Mr. Bellingham, "we have important business to discuss with him."

"I regret," said the Egyptian, "that Mr. Washington himself sees no one. At any rate, he sees no one on their first visit here. It falls to the lot of his subordinates—among which I have the honour to be numbered—to talk to clients in the first instance, and see if their business is of sufficient importance to merit his working on it personally. You understand," he went on with a bland wave of his hand, "that we do not take on all business indiscriminately. We only accept those cases where it seems that there is some likelihood of a miscarriage of justice occurring if we do not step in."

"Does all this rigmarole mean that we can't see the principal of this agency?" asked Mr. Bellingham aggressively.

"I regret that it does," returned the other.

"Then," said Mr. Bellingham, "I'm sorry what we have to leave you. I never deal with subordinates."

"I, too, am sorry, Mr. Bellingham," said the Egyptian, "if you cannot trust me with your business. I think that Miss Latimer and yourself will find me quite discreet."

"How the devil did you know our names?" spluttered Mr. Bellingham.

"It is, my dear sir, our business here to know things. I think," said the Egyptian, "that many people would be somewhat unpleasantly surprised if they realised all that we know. But that, needless to say, does not apply to honoured clients such as yourselves." Margery wondered if it was pure fancifulness on her part, or did the Egyptian really permit a sarcastic smile to flit across his countenance at that last sentence?

"At any rate," he continued, "you will at least do me the honour of coming into my humble study and telling me a little of what is troubling you. Unless, of course, you prefer that I should call at your house one evening? I can do so easily if you should prefer it to be done that way."

"No, no!" said Mr. Bellingham hurriedly, and Margery stared at him, surprised at his vehemence. "We'll come in, and tell you about it now, if you don't mind," he went on, and the Oriental bowed impressively, and held open the door of the inner room from which he had emerged to greet them.

As they walked in Margery looked around her curiously. The room did not strike her as being at all like the typical detective's study of fiction. There was a large roll-top desk, it is true, and a revolving chair behind it. And there were two comfortable armchairs, towards which the Egyptian waved his hand, indicating that they were to seat themselves therein.

But apart from this there was little to suggest the grim business of detection. On the walls were some dainty little watercolours, executed mainly in cream and sepia. Probably Egyptian work, Margery decided. And there were a few books on a shelf just opposite the roll-top desk, which Margery managed to make out as cheap editions of modern fiction—but not detective stories. A very unorthodox detective, certainly!

"Now," said Mr. Bellingham, "I wonder if you will give me your name. It's very difficult talking to someone whose name you don't know."

"I regret," said the Egyptian, "that we are not permitted to state our names. In any case, I am, as no doubt you have perceived, not an Englishman, and I believe that English people find some difficulty in pronouncing my Egyptian name." Margery congratulated herself. She had "spotted" his nationality rightly, then!

"Well, what am I to call you, then?" asked Mr. Bellingham.

"Does not your immortal Lewis Carroll somewhere say: 'He answered to "Hi!" or to any loud cry'?" asked the Egyptian, "very well, that, my dear Mr. Bellingham, is like my humble self. Though if at any time you wish to come here again, and to consult me, you may give my number. I am number fifty-six on the roll of Washington detectives."

"I suppose that we shall have to leave it at that," said Mr. Bellingham grumblingly, "but it doesn't seem very satisfactory to me."

"Yes," said the Egyptian, "many of our clients do not seem to like this anonymity. But, believe me, it is all done with the best of motives. And now, my dear Mr. Bellingham and my dear Miss Latimer, may I have your stories?"

Mr. Bellingham took the lead. First of all he told all that was publicly known of the murder. Then he went on to detail the facts which he had assembled about the disappearance of John

Cook. And finally he turned to Margery, asking her if there were any important things which he had omitted to mention.

"One, and one only, Mr. Bellingham," she said, "and that you did not know. No one knew it but myself and one other. It is this that I think our friend"—and she bowed slightly to the Egyptian, who bowed in return—"that our friend should know, and that is that John Cook was seen to emerge from Sir Henry Henshaw's car shortly after the murder."

"Good Heavens!" said Mr. Bellingham, "how do you know that, Margery?"

"Because I saw him," answered Margery, "but I haven't told the police yet, as I'm afraid that they might construe it as another point in the case against him."

"Thank you, madame," said the Egyptian, "I can assure you that I appreciate your confidence and that it will be not abused."

"But. . . but. . . doesn't this make it fairly certain that Cook is. . . is. . .?" stammered Mr. Bellingham.

"Is the murderer of all these unfortunate men?" said the Egyptian.

"That was what I meant," said Mr. Bellingham.

The Egyptian thought for a moment. "I am not so sure about that," he said, "although I must admit that things do look rather black against him. Let us consider the facts for a moment. What Miss Latimer has just told us shows that he was there on the occasion of the first murder, or very soon after it. He was, you tell me, Mr. Bellingham, in your office only a very few minutes before you discovered the body of Lord Chaney. Again you saw him, or thought you saw him, in Slough, only a few minutes before the third murder. As to the last murder, he has not, perhaps, been very definitely connected with that, but it seems fairly certain, from what you tell me about Williamson's message to Miss Latimer, that he had every reason to do away with the man, even if he were not being blackmailed by him, which seems only too likely."

"A pretty damning indictment, isn't it?" queried Mr. Bellingham.

"I have not finished yet, Mr. Bellingham," said the Egyptian, "there is the question of motive to be considered. You tell me that Mr. Cook is the founder and president of the National Anti-Speed Association, the main principles of which are related to the evils of the speed mania so typical of the present day. He was, it seems, practically a monomaniac himself on the point. All the men who have been murdered, save only the fourth one, which case I have already explained, are prominent in the world where speed and speed records are the most important things."

"Then you think that Mr. Cook is guilty," faltered Margery.

"I did not say so, my dear Miss Latimer," said the Egyptian, his face creasing into a kindly smile, "I am only trying to suggest to you what the counsel for the prosecution would say if this case ever came to court."

"What do you really think about it?" asked Margery.

"That, I fear, would not be politic for me to tell you at the moment," he returned, "but I am trying to point out that there are dangers if we find Mr. Cook. It is quite possible that the police would wish to arrest him immediately he was found."

"But I thought that you always made a principle of working according to the law," interjected Mr. Bellingham, "and if a man was wanted by the police you always made a habit of giving him up to them."

"That is so," admitted the Egyptian, "if he is guilty of the crime or crimes for which the police wish to arrest him. But otherwise—no. We do not assist, as I said at the beginning of our interview, at miscarriages of justice. We only assist when we think that our intervention will prevent such a miscarriage from taking place."

"But John Cook is innocent!" exclaimed Margery.

"That, my dear young lady," said the Egyptian tranquilly, "is as it may be. The fact remains that the police in all probability think him guilty. And if they arrest him and prove their case against him to the satisfaction of twelve idiots who are called a jury, he will be hanged, innocent or not."

"We don't hang innocent men in this country!" was Mr. Bellingham's contribution to the conversation at this point.

"Don't we?" The Egyptian smiled, but it was not a pleasant smile this time. "My friend, if you knew how many innocent people had been hanged during this last twenty years, you would not sleep soundly in that so comfortable bed of yours tonight."

"Well, what do you recommend us to do?" asked Margery, her head buzzing round with the discussion. It seemed, she thought, hopeless to expect anything tangible to come from all this talk.

"That is for you to decide," answered the Egyptian, "for if you think Mr. Cook guilty and wish him to be caught, we shall catch him for you. If you think him guilty and wish him to escape, you had better not give us the case. If, on the other hand, you think him innocent, his being found might clear up many misunderstandings."

"Find him!" said Margery impulsively, "he is innocent of these crimes, I am sure, and when you have found him I know that he will be able to explain everything."

"I wish that I shared your faith, my dear," said Mr. Bellingham, "but I, too, think that our friend had better do what he can towards tracing Mr. Cook. Unless he is found, it seems certain that these dastardly crimes will never be cleared up."

"Then you wish us to proceed?" asked the Egyptian.

"Yes," answered Margery and Mr. Bellingham together.

"Very well," he said, "and I trust that we shall have some news for you within a day or two."

He bowed and opened the door to them. They proceeded into the outer room, and, walking across to the door into the corridor, they saw it open slowly at their approach.

As they were walking out into the corridor, Margery turned round for a moment, and saw, as she expected, that the

136

door leading into the room of the Egyptian was again quite invisible.

It must be let into the wall in some way.

The lift was waiting for them, and it wafted them down to the ground floor in the same mysterious fashion.

Within less than five minutes of leaving the strange Egyptian, they were in the Underground train again. And it was not until they got there that Margery permitted herself to speak.

"Tell me, Mr. Bellingham," she said, "did that man think John Cook guilty or innocent?"

"I don't know, I'm sure," he said, "but I can tell you one thing, Margery. If he's guilty or if he's innocent, now that we've put George Washington on his track, John Cook will be found!"

CHAPTER XVI

THE LETTER

A DOLPHUS was sitting despondently on the stairs outside the office. Miss Latimer, he thought, must have been spirited away by the same mysterious agency that caused the boss to disappear. For one fleeting moment he saw himself, Sherlock Holmes, Sexton Blake and all the other detectives of his youthful reading rolled into one, but the dream was soon dispelled by the appearance of Miss Latimer herself.

"Why, hullo, Adolphus," she said, with that pleasant smile of hers, "did you think that I was lost?"

"Well, miss," he mumbled, "I was beginning to wonder, like. . ."

"Good job that you didn't send for the police, then," she returned, fitting her key into the door meanwhile, "or they would have been mad with you when they realised that we were both of us quite safe."

"Both of you, miss?" Adolphus could hardly believe his ears. "Do you mean the boss and yourself?"

"Who else, Adolphus?" Margery was in the seventh heaven of delight. That was obvious even to the not particularly observant eyes and ears of the office boy.

"Well, miss, I can only say that I'm real glad," he said, "and when shall we see the boss back here at work again?"

"That I can't say Adolphus," returned Margery, "but I don't think that the present state of affairs will go on for very long."

And she passed inwards to her own office, leaving a very pleased and very puzzled Adolphus to sit down and try to think things out.

When she was at her desk, the typewriter before her, she opened her hand-bag and took out the letter once more. This letter she had only read a few moments before, but it had given her a greater degree of real happiness than she had known for many a day.

She had left Mr. Bellingham in Chancery Lane, whilst she strolled down to her place in Fleet Street. She had opened her hand-bag to take out a handkerchief, and there, reposing amongst the muddle of powder-puff, safety pins, cigarette case and all the rest, was this letter, a welcome intruder.

At first she had thought it something forgotten, a letter which should have been posted but had somehow been overlooked, but a glance at its address had disabused her of that notion. "Margery" was all that it said, and the word was written in a familiar handwriting which made her heart jump painfully. It was a letter from John! How it had found its mysterious way into her hand-bag she did not care. It was sufficient that it had made its appearance.

Careless of observation she had torn the flap with a trembling hand, and then, standing on the pavement of Fleet Street, she had read it.

"Margery dear," it had begun, and the intimacy of the words had almost brought tears of joy to her eyes. And then it went on to say, "I am writing this to let you know that you mustn't worry. I am quite safe, and shall, before very long, come back to you. At the moment it is impossible that you should be told any more. I am sorry to keep things from you, but as I said when last we met, the secret is not my own to tell. Others share it, and until they are safe I cannot tell you more.

"You will, I know, understand what I say. But above all things do not tell anyone at all, not even Mr. Bellingham or Inspector Shelley, about this letter. They might be able to find me before I am ready. And that would never do.

"Au revoir, my dear. Yours ever, John."

That was all. But for Margery it was quite enough. It meant that John was safe, that one day he would soon clear himself of this wretched web of suspicion and distrust which had been woven around him, and that then he would come for her and they would be happy together.

As she sat at her desk there, reading the letter through again and again, Margery felt more cheerful than she had for some time. Her future looked comparatively hopeful. Of course, she knew well that there must be all sorts of difficulties to be surmounted—otherwise, why this secrecy?—but she felt absolutely confident that John was capable of overcoming them.

But how did the letter come to be in her hand-bag? She could only remember one occasion when it had left her grasp, even for a moment, and that was when they had been talking to the Egyptian in the offices of "George Washington, Ltd." Surely the letter could not have been inserted into her bag then? It would be too dangerous, even if John had managed to convey it in some secret way to the Egyptian. And yet, how else. . .? Margery was frankly puzzled at the whole thing.

Just, however, as she was beginning to think that the question would have to be left until she saw John, when no doubt he would be able to explain the whole business, Adolphus tapped discreetly at the door and entered, followed by a familiar figure—the figure of Detective-Inspector Shelley.

Shelley looked haggard and worn, as if the strain of this complicated case were beginning to tell on him.

"You look tired, Inspector," said Margery kindly.

"I am," he said simply, "but that can't be helped at the moment. We're close on the heels of the criminal in this confounded case. Before many hours I think that we shall have him."

"Do you mean John Cook?" asked Margery, surprised at her own temerity in thus carrying the battle into the enemy's country.

"I fear that I can't answer that question just yet," said Shelley, with a weary smile, "but I will tell you this, Miss Latimer.

When we make our arrest, you and some other people will be considerably surprised."

Margery was again puzzled. This man seemed to speak in enigmas. He was not a straightforward man, such as John Cook. When you were talking to him, you always got the impression that he was keeping something hidden, something, to speak metaphorically, up his sleeve. Margery did not altogether like it, but she felt quite certain that he was absolutely honest and scrupulously fair, even to the unfortunates whom it was his duty to arrest.

"But surely you did not come here to tell me this," said Margery, "you don't really mean to say that you are so sorry for me that you wish to end my misery at the earliest possible moment." The radiant smile which spread over her face as she spoke effectually disproved the sentiments which she expressed.

"Partly yes and partly no, must be my answer to that question," replied the detective, "the other reason why I came round here was to ask you one simple question."

"And that is. . .?" said Margery.

"That is," said the detective stolidly, "why it is necessary for you to go behind the backs of the official police and consult some hole-in-a-corner private detective about this affair?"

"However did you know that we had been to see George Washington?" asked Margery.

"George Fiddlesticks!" exclaimed the detective warmly, "why, you don't think that we let you roam about London unprotected, do you? When you have been involved in a case which quite certainly has a particularly nasty kind of killer in it? But, look here, you said 'we' consulted that fathead of a George Washington? Who was the gentleman? The man who was trailing you that day did not know him."

"It was Mr. Bellingham, if you really wish to know," said Margery, with some hauteur, "but I should like to point out to you, Mr. Shelley, that I have no particular desire to stroll around London with a detective on my heels."

"A detective on your heels is better than a knife in your back," retorted the Scotland Yard man, "what you have to remember, young lady, is that this man, the man we shall arrest shortly, is not just an ordinary person like you or like myself. He is a killer. He has killed four men, and if he gets it into his head that you have information which might convict him, he will kill you in the same way! Don't you realise that?" His words were serious enough, in all conscience, but Margery somehow got the impression that he was talking to cover some emotion or other, possibly surprise at the fact that Mr. Bellingham had accompanied her to the office of the private detectives.

"You noted, I hope," said Margery, trying to penetrate his mental armour, "that it was only Mr. Bellingham who went with me to see those people?"

"I did," he said curtly, and instantly changed the subject.

"Tell me one thing more," he said, "what do you think that you can gain from consulting these people? Their job is shadowing suspects in divorce cases and such like unsavoury work."

"I should think, Mr. Shelley," said Margery, "that you should know by now that these people are not like that. They make a special point of helping the law when the law looks like going astray."

"Helping my grandmother!" said Shelley irritably. Probably, Margery thought, the pressure of work in this case was having its effect on his temper.

He had nothing more to say, however, and soon Margery was left alone again with her thoughts.

The knowledge that she was being followed every time that she went out was new to her. She had, it was true, once or twice observed a stranger who seemed to be, in spite of his strangeness, in some vague way known to her, but she had told herself that he was probably an assistant in some shop where she was in the habit of buying. Probably he had been a detective! For some reason the thought made her feel somewhat uneasy. It is never pleasant to feel that one's actions are under constant observation, and to one placed as was Margery, keeping something back from the police, it was doubly distasteful.

Anyhow, she would have to make the best of it, she decided. There was, in all probability, no way of getting rid of this man who was shadowing her. He was quite certainly too much of an expert at his job for her to have any chance of throwing him off the trail.

Adolphus entered once more. "A gentleman, miss," he announced. He was very excited, and Margery wondered who the visitor could be.

"What is his name, Adolphus?" she asked.

"He wouldn't say, miss," said Adolphus, "but he is a foreign gentleman, and he said that if I told you number fifty-six was here, you would understand."

Fifty-six! That was the Egyptian at the detective agency! Why, it was only about an hour and a half since she had left him. Surely he could not have news for her already.

"Show him in, Adolphus," she said resolutely.

The Egyptian entered silently, looking around him like one who is not quite sure of his ground.

"Miss Latimer, I am honoured," he said, bowing low over the hand which she held out to him.

"Won't you sit down, and tell me the reason for your visit?" she asked.

"I thank you," he said, and sank into the depths of the chair which she offered him.

Neither of them spoke a word for some thirty seconds, and then, without preamble, the Egyptian embarked on his story.

"We have," he said, "succeeded in tracing Mr. Cook. It was not really difficult for us, although," he added, with a smile, "it is easy to comprehend that the police found it a somewhat troublesome task."

"Where is he?" asked Margery breathlessly.

"That, I fear, Miss Latimer, I cannot tell you," he replied, "although I hope that within a very short time I shall have the pleasure of leading you to him. It is essential, however, that you should reach him secretly, without any other person knowing where you have gone."

"Is he in danger?" This was the question which was uppermost in Margery's mind.

"Not at present," said the Egyptian gravely, "but if certain people were to get upon his track very great danger might threaten him. That is why such secrecy is necessary for you to get to him."

"Shall I get Mr. Bellingham?" she asked.

"No," said the other, "you must get no one and tell no one. You must come to him with such secrecy that all your friends will think, for a time at any rate, that you have disappeared. That, I am afraid, is the only way that you can hope to save yourself and him from the danger which may threaten you both."

"But there is a Scotland Yard man who follows me all the time," said Margery.

"That," said the Egyptian with a smile, "was not unknown to us. But all that will be arranged. I wish you to receive your instructions from me. Then, if you carry them out perfectly, you will be with Mr. Cook by this evening."

"What am I to do?" Margery could hardly contain her excitement as she asked the question.

"Listen carefully." The Egyptian was clearly repeating something which he had learned by rote. "Tonight, when you are in your room, at nine-thirty precisely a person will knock gently at the door. Three short knocks, and then an interval. Three more short knocks. Like this." And he tapped gently on the desk in the manner he had described.

"I see," said Margery, "what then?"

"You will let her in," he said, "it will be a young lady of about your own age. You are not to be surprised by anything in

144

her appearance. You will allow her to dress you in the clothes which she will bring and you will allow her to alter your appearance in the manner which she desires. Then, she will go.

You will wait for ten minutes exactly. Not more, not less. When she has gone for that time, you will go gently downstairs, trying not to arouse any attention, and you will go to the cab rank just off the Queen's Road. It is near the Bayswater Underground Station, just down a side-road a little way. You know it?"

Margery nodded. She was all aglow with excitement. This, obviously, was a well-thought out plan for throwing the detectives off her track.

"Then," he continued, "you will take the first cab on the rank. You need not say anything to the driver. He will know where to go. Within less than half an hour from the time that you get into that cab you will be with Mr. Cook. Where he is, I have told you I cannot say. As a matter of fact, I do not yet know myself, although I shall know by this evening. My only instructions were to tell you to do as I bid. Is that perfectly clear to you?"

Carefully, step by step, Margery rehearsed what the Egyptian had told her, and only when she was word-perfect was he satisfied.

"It is well," he announced at length, "I shall now bid you au revoir, Miss Latimer. Before this evening is over I hope that I shall have the pleasure of meeting you again. But remember: tell no one of this, not even Mr. Bellingham or your so kind Mr. Shelley."

And noiselessly as he had come, he had gone again. Margery sat in her chair motionless for many minutes after his departure, going over in her mind all that he had said. The imperative need for complete secrecy she saw. If Shelley were to know about this, the police would be on the trail of John Cook. And that might well prove fatal. His letter had announced that he would shortly be able to clear himself of all suspicion. But at the moment, she supposed that he had not sufficient evidence for that.

So she must keep quite silent about this. She felt sorry for Adolphus and for Mr. Bellingham. They would both, she thought, be very worried when she disappeared. But it would not be for long. Soon this terrifying mystery would be cleared up, and then they could all be happy together.

CHAPTER XVII

MARGERY ESCAPES

THE remainder of the time which had, somehow, to be gone through, dragged for Margery as no time in her life had ever done before.

She thought that the time to leave the office and go home would never arrive. And when she was in her room in Bayswater once again, she thought that the laggard hours between six o'clock and half-past nine seemed the longest three and a half hours that she had ever known.

Just as a church clock outside had struck the half hour, however, she heard a gentle tap on her door. They were very prompt, these gentry, whoever they might be! Margery opened the door, and a girl stepped daintily in. She was wearing a long coat, and one of those floppy hats which hide most of one's countenance. She had the thick fur collar of the coat turned well up around her neck, so that practically nothing of her face could be seen. Also, as Margery noted with amazement, the coat was of a very hideous mustard-yellow colour, whilst the hat was bright green.

But her amazement at her visitor's attire was nothing to the amazement which she felt when the girl removed her hat and coat. She gazed at her visitor spellbound. The girl was a literal and absolute double of herself! It was like looking into a mirror, except that the clothes did not correspond.

"Pretty good, isn't it?" said the girl, in a pleasant voice. "It's wonderful what a little grease-paint and a spot of talent for altering one's expression will do." As if to show what she meant, she relaxed her face and Margery saw that there was really only a resemblance to her own.

"I had a certain likeness to begin with, of course," said the girl, "otherwise it couldn't be done. And now I must start to work on you."

"What are you going to do?" asked Margery.

"My instructions were to alter your appearance as much as I could in a few minutes," answered the other, "and I don't think that it will be particularly difficult. You see, a touch or two with a razor and a few spots of paint will make you very different. Got a towel?"

Margery turned away to get the required article, and when she turned back she saw that her visitor had her hand-bag open, and was producing from it, like a magician produces rabbits from a hat, a small razor, sticks of grease-paint, and other articles which were complete mysteries to Margery's mind.

"Lock the door," said the girl, "and keep quiet." Margery had no option but to obey, wondering all the while what exactly was the scheme. It seemed to be well thought out, at any rate.

The girl started on Margery's eyebrows. "They won't take long to grow right again," she said reassuringly. She tucked the towel well under Margery's chin, and took up the little razor. With a few deft touches she removed the outer ends of the brows, and then, with a charcoal pencil, continued them inwards towards the nose, pausing every now and then to look at her handiwork, and see if it met with approval.

Then she took up some sticks of grease-paint, and set to work at the cheeks. A few dabs here and there, and a rubbing in with nimble fingers, followed by a scattering of powder and more rubbing, was the process here.

Finally she requested Margery to open her mouth, produced some queer-looking black stuff from a packet, and did some mysterious business with her teeth. And then, she looked at Margery with some pleasure.

"I think that will do," she announced at length, "a pretty hurried job, but not so bad, all the same, it seems to me."

She handed Margery a mirror, and Margery looked into it with some interest. Good Heavens! she thought, surely this could not be her? The girl at whom she was gazing had thick black eyebrows, almost meeting at the middle, a red complexion, with that peculiar lined redness usually associated with the gypsies, and, when she opened her mouth, she saw that it looked as if two or three of the more prominent of her teeth were gone. There was a gap in the centre of the upper jaw.

The face, in fact, was the face of a stranger! So much had been done by a few minutes' skilled work.

"It's marvellous!" she said, "I should never have believed such a thing to be possible."

"Oh, if I'd had time, I could have done much better than that," said the girl with a laugh, "but there was no time to make you look older, for instance, or anything of that sort. By the way, all this will come off easily enough. Rub your face with cold cream and then wash thoroughly in warm water. The tooth stuff will come off easily if you clean your teeth in the ordinary way."

"But what is the idea of all this?" Margery was quite frankly puzzled by it.

"I thought that you knew all that," said the girl, "it's simple enough, anyhow. I shall dress in your hat and coat, and shall go outside, standing about to attract the attention of any policeman or detective who happens to be about. Then I shall take a taxi and drive off into the wilderness of Golder's Green or Hammersmith or somewhere, whilst the detective will be bound to follow me. You will be free from supervision, and will be able to go where you wish without being followed."

"Then why all this disguise?" asked Margery.

"Oh, that!" The girl laughed again. "That's just a little precaution. You see, if anyone who knows you happened to see me getting into the taxi, and then, a few minutes later, saw you come out of the house, he would begin to think that there was something very fishy about things."

"And you really think that it will work?"

"Of course it will! There's not a flaw in the plan anywhere as far as I can see," asserted her visitor confidently, "when George Washington works a thing, that thing succeeds, believe me." And she shook her head a little impatiently.

"Who is George Washington?" asked Margery, a little curiously. Ever since her first introduction to the remarkable detective agency she had wanted an answer to this question.

"My dear Miss Latimer," said the girl, "if you know anything at all about my job—and I think that you know quite a lot—you must know that I should get the sack tomorrow if I let you have any notion about who my boss really is. His real name is never used, even amongst ourselves. And to use it when talking to a client would just about finish any one of us."

Margery sighed. It seemed as if this was one of the many things in connection with the remarkable events which she had come across which would remain a mystery, at any rate.

"And now," said her visitor, glancing at the watch which was on her dainty wrist, "it is time that I went. You know what you have to do, don't you? Wait ten minutes, and then, wearing that perfectly hideous hat and coat which I wore, you will go out and take the cab which has been placed there for you?"

"I know," said Margery, "but may I ask one thing more?"

"Ask away," said the other, "although I don't guarantee that I shall answer, you know. Might be another rather indiscreet question. Ugh," she grunted, before Margery had time to answer her request, "why are you so small? No joke trying to get into a coat two inches too small for you." She was, indeed, finding it a mighty struggle to get into Margery's coat. But she managed it at last, and buttoned it up determinedly.

"Now," she said, "that question?"

"Why," asked Margery, "is it necessary that I should dress in such a particularly lurid costume?" And she pointed at the yellow coat and green hat which her visitor had thrown carelessly over a chair.

"Another precaution," answered her visitor. "If any curious persons saw me come, and didn't see me come out again, there would be trouble. Chitter-chatter. Gossip. You know the sort of thing I mean. Girl in bilious coat and green hat is seen to go into the beautiful Miss Latimer's flat, or apartment or whatever you call this place. Girl in bilious coat and green hat seen to come out again, everything's O.K. The fact that it's a different girl doesn't matter. Curious person isn't to know that. Get me, Steve?"

"Yes, I think I see," said Margery. "That's all then."

"That's all," said the remarkable visitor, "and so I'll say cheerio. Don't forget to lock the door after I'm gone. Might be a bit awkward if you were asked to explain your presence in your own room."

And she was gone, swiftly as her words. Margery hurriedly crossed the room, locked the door and settled down to pass the ten minutes which, per instructions, had to pass before she was allowed to leave the room.

The time dragged, as all time does under such circumstances. But eventually it went, and then Margery dressed herself in the hat and coat which the visitor had left, shuddering at the atrocious combination of colours which had been chosen as likely to stick in an observant person's memory.

Fortunately she did not meet anyone going down the stairs. If she had met Jean McKean, her own particular friend, or any other of the many friends with whom she had spent pleasant hours in the past, she did not know what she would have done. But still, she reflected, that would not matter: they would never know her in her present disguise.

Once in the street the rest was simple. She made her way into Queen's Road, and strolled along to the cab-rank which the Egyptian had described to her. Indeed, she needed no description. The place was well known to her. Although she had never had money to throw away on cabs, she used the Underground railway with some regularity, and this cab-rank, as the Egyptian had said, was very near the Bayswater underground station.

Still following instructions, she walked up to the rank, and paused beside the first taxi there. The driver had his head more or less within contact with the engine. The bonnet was up, and he was listening to the engine, which was "ticking over," as if he felt something was wrong.

She soon saw, however, that this was only subterfuge. Obviously something like this would have to be done, in case any other would-be traveller had required a taxi before she arrived on the spot.

At her arrival the driver slammed down the bonnet with remarkable celerity, and muttered "That's better" to himself, but clearly for the benefit of any other driver who might happen to be within hearing distance.

"Cab, lady?" he said, touching his cap.

"Ye-es," said Margery, rather doubtfully.

"That's all right, lady," he replied, "jump in." Margery jumped. And, as he shut the door after her, the driver murmured to her, reassuringly, "It's all right, miss. I know who you are and where I have to take you."

Margery felt considerably relieved. It did not, indeed, surprise her, that the voice with which he had spoken was quite different from the voice which he had been using before. Then it had been a rough Cockney tone, the tone of the usual taxi-driver. Now it was something more cultured, the tone of one who had seen the colleges of Oxford from the inside.

Soon they were rattling away through the familiar streets of Bayswater, and on towards Paddington. Margery saw the approach of the Great Western terminus, and the lights of the streets around it, streets which had always been familiar to her since her first arrival in London from the West Country.

Then, with startling suddenness the change came. She was looking out at the streets, just beyond the station, wondering which way they would go next, when she could see no more.

The taxi had suddenly turned into a box. Shutters had slid up outside the windows, as she found when she lowered one of the windows to find out what had happened.

For a moment she was left in absolute darkness, and then a light shone out of the roof. This was indeed a remarkable taxi!

"What is the meaning of this?" she said to the driver, using the speaking tube which had been provided for the purpose.

"Sorry, Miss Latimer," he said, still speaking in that curiously refined voice of his, "my instructions were that you were not to know where you were being taken. Pity that I had to do it, but what would you have?" She could imagine that she saw him shrugging his shoulders as he spoke.

"How long is this farce to be kept up?" she asked angrily, knowing that she could do nothing to help.

"It's not a farce, I'm afraid," he replied, "it's deadly serious. But you will come to no harm. It is just that the chief thinks it safer for you and for everyone else concerned that you should not know where you are being taken tonight." And he lapsed into silence again.

Margery listened intently to the sounds which penetrated into her prison (for so she thought of it) from outside. For a while she could hear nothing, but then she heard the sounds of the traffic, which seemed to be becoming steadily louder. They were doubtless approaching the city—or at least the West End, full of bustle and noise now, with the theatre traffic.

This continued for some minutes, and then it began to get quieter again. Somewhere on the north of London, she decided, since they had clearly gone through the busy part of the metropolis, and were now approaching a part where the traffic was thinning out once more.

Then she heard an engine whistle, and the roar of a train passing near by. Where could it be? Liverpool Street, King's Cross, Euston, St. Pancras? Mentally she went over the stations of the north and east. But she could not possibly decide which it was. Probably a suburban station, since they had apparently left the busy streets behind. And, like most Londoners, Margery knew little of the suburbs.

At last the cab came to a standstill, and the driver came round and opened the door.

"I'm very glad, Miss Latimer," he said, as he helped her to alight, "that you didn't try to open the door and jump out. As a matter of fact, it would be impossible, as this taxi has a self-locking door, worked from the driving seat. But it might have made some trouble. You see, I didn't want you to start shouting or anything, as it might have attracted unnecessary attention to us."

Meanwhile Margery was gazing around her curiously. She was in a street of tall houses, and the yellow glow of the lamps shaded off into the indefiniteness of the middle distance. She was still in London, but where? She had not the remotest idea.

"I suppose it would be useless to ask you where I am?" she said.

"Quite useless," he admitted gravely, "as I am under orders to answer no questions. This way, please." And he led her up some steps and into one of the dull-looking houses.

CHAPTER XVIII

MORE PUZZLES FOR SHELLEY

SHELLEY was very pleased with life.

This case, which at first had seemed only too complicated was, he thought, beginning to straighten out at last. He was beginning to see daylight, and hoped to make an arrest within a few days at most.

But before that desirable event could occur, there were several things which badly wanted doing. Gaps in his knowledge would have to be filled up, questions answered and more evidence put together. However, he did not doubt that it would be done, and he reassured the Chief Commissioner, who was getting rather worried about the case, as indeed he had every reason for doing.

The first person to be seen was Margery Latimer. Now that his case was beginning to assume a reasonable shape, Shelley thought that he would be able to make that annoying young lady talk on subjects which she had hitherto refused to broach.

So, on the morning following the events recorded in the previous chapter, Shelley called in at the office in Crane Court. It was comparatively early when he arrived there—about ten o'clock, to be precise, but he knew that Margery had a way of arriving at a fairly early hour.

He was therefore very surprised to see a somewhat tearful Adolphus sitting disconsolately on the step outside the office door.

"Why, what's the trouble, young man?" he asked cheerfully.

"Miss Latimer ain't come in this morning, that's what the trouble is," answered Adolphus with a sniff, "and it's my opinion, Mr. Shelley, that they've got her at last."

"Who've got her?" asked Shelley sharply. Surely, he thought, with success almost within his grasp, the enemy had not succeeded in getting Margery!

"Them as took the boss away," replied Adolphus, "and if you ask me, Mr. Shelley, we shan't never see neither of 'em again." Having emitted this doleful pronouncement, Adolphus burst, unashamedly, into tears.

"This won't do, now, this won't do," said Shelley, "you've got to buck up, young man, and tell me all you know about the business. Why, for all you know, Miss Latimer may have a headache, and be merely staying in bed for a few hours until she feels better."

"That's all very well, sir," said the boy, raising his head, and looking at Shelley with miserable eyes, "but if so, why didn't she let me know? She knows my address all right, and if she wasn't coming to the office I know that she'd let me know. It's that there blooming foreigner, that's who it is."

"Look here, Adolphus," said Shelley, taking a firm grip of the boy's shoulders and shaking him severely, "you will have to tell me what you know about this. Who the foreigner is and all that sort of thing, you know. But we shall save time if you tell me about it in the car. We'll run along to Miss Latimer's lodging, and then, if it's still necessary, back to Scotland Yard. Then we shall be getting something done, and you will be telling me all about it at the same time."

In the car, *en route* for Bayswater, Adolphus described the visit of the Egyptian the day before, but Shelley could make little of it. He was not acquainted with all the staff of George Washington, nor did he know who might be calling at the office with business genuinely connected with the National Anti-Speed Association. For the moment, therefore, he dismissed Adolphus's suspicions of this foreign gentleman as absurd, though pigeonholing a description of the visitor in his mind—for future reference, as it were.

Soon they arrived at Margery's Bayswater home, and here they learned that Adolphus had some basis for his fears, after all.

Fortunately enough, they found Jean McKean at home.

She, as a particular friend of the missing girl, could naturally provide them with much information.

"I went into her room last night, Mr. Shelley," she said, "it must have been a short time after ten o'clock. She wasn't there then, I know. But I'd seen her only about an hour before, when she came along to my room to return a book she'd borrowed."

"Between nine and ten, then, you think that she left the house," said Shelley thoughtfully.

"It would seem like that wouldn't it?" returned the girl. "That's how it appears to me, I must say," she added unnecessarily, "although, of course, she might have strolled out to the post or something, and finally left the house at some later time still."

"Don't think so, Miss McKean," said Shelley gruffly, "'twould be straining coincidence too much. I think it's pretty certain that Miss Latimer left this house between nine and ten last night, and that, as your landlady has told me, she didn't return, and hasn't returned up to this moment."

This was really all the information that Jean McKean had to give them, and Shelley thought it would be worthwhile having a look at Margery's room before finally leaving the house.

Adolphus had followed all the investigations with the keen-eyed interest of a boy raised on Sexton Blake and his colleagues, and now he was genuinely thrilled. To think that he was actually helping a real Scotland Yard detective in a real criminal hunt!

"What do you think's happened, sir?" he asked eagerly.

"Can't say," was Shelley's curt reply, "but it looks as if there was something in your suspicions, Adolphus, my lad."

In Margery's neat little bed-sitting room Shelley learned little. To the surprise of Adolphus, he did not crawl about on his stomach, examining the carpet with a large magnifying glass. He did not even attempt to examine the shiny places on the furniture with a view to finding finger-prints.

"But is this all you do, sir?" asked Adolphus at last, unable to contain his disappointment any longer.

"Not showy enough for you, I suppose," commented the detective with a smile, "well," he added, pouncing on a small object on the floor, "here's something for you to exercise your wits on, my lad. What is this doing on the floor of Miss Latimer's bed-sitting-room?"

"What is it?" asked Adolphus, all eager interest.

For answer the detective drew the object across the back of his hand. It left a red mark where it had passed.

"Grease-paint?" asked Adolphus, and Shelley nodded.

"Right first time," he said, "but the point, Adolphus my lad, is that Miss Latimer did not use paint of any kind, and, even if she did, this is definitely actor's grease-paint, which is used for altering the appearance of your face. What do you think is the answer to the riddle now, Adolphus?"

"An actor is in it," answered the boy without a moment's hesitation, "p'raps he's the bloke what kidnapped her."

"Ever hear of an actor carrying odd sticks of grease-paint about in his pocket?" Shelley pursued, "no, my lad, you'll have to think out a better answer than that. But before we go, I'd better make sure on that point."

Jean McKean was quite sure that Margery did not use paint of any kind on her face. A little powder, that was all. She had never seen this stick of grease-paint before, and she did not know of any actors or actresses among Margery's friends.

"And if she had any friends who were actors or actresses, Mr. Shelley," she added, "you can be sure that I should have known them. Her friends were my friends, as the frothblowers used to sing." And she giggled.

"Did you know Mr. John Cook?" asked Shelley, and left her standing open-mouthed. He felt rather pleased with that last remark, for he was sure that whatever else Margery might have told Jean, she would not have shared with her the knowledge of John Cook's whereabouts. And Shelley liked to puzzle people. He said it was a detective's prerogative.

"Back to Scotland Yard," he told the chauffeur, and then settled back in his seat in a brown study, from which even the eager, excited eyes of Adolphus could not draw him.

When they arrived, he curtly ordered Adolphus to follow him, and proceeded to his room.

He took up the telephone, and spoke, still curtly, various orders down it. Then "Is Stuart back?" he asked. The answer apparently was satisfactory, for "Send him up right away," he said, and slammed down the receiver hard.

"Now, Adolphus," he told the boy, "this man who is coming in here is a detective who has been following Miss Latimer. He was outside her lodging last night, and he'll be able to tell us what has happened to her."

The man who came in did not look like Adolphus's idea of a detective, any more than Shelley himself did. He had flaming red hair, and he was nearly six feet in height. In fact, a more noticeable specimen of humanity it would have been impossible to imagine. It was therefore a great testimony to his ability that Margery had not found his presence troublesome, or, indeed, particularly obtrusive.

"Stuart," said Shelley, "this is the young man who reported Miss Latimer's disappearance. I want to know where she's gone. Quick, man, we've no time to lose."

Stuart looked rather sheepish. "The fact is, sir," he faltered, "she gave me the slip last night."

"Gave you the slip! You!" Shelley was really astonished. "I thought that you were the best shadow we have at the Yard," he said.

"I thought so too, sir," said the man with a rather self-conscious grin, "but that young lady was one too many for me, sir. I'll tell you how it happened."

"Yes, do," said Shelley savagely, "it will be a most amusing experience for us, especially as Miss Latimer was a most crucial witness in a murder case."

"I'm very sorry, sir," said Stuart, flushing scarlet under this sarcasm, "but I'm sure that the trick she played would have beaten anyone. If you'd been on her trail, sir, she would have done you just the same."

"Thank you for the compliment, Stuart," said Shelley, "but get on with your story. This is Scotland Yard, you know, not a mutual admiration society."

"Very good, sir," answered Stuart, "Miss Latimer, sir, left the house at a quarter to ten last night. It is, I imagine, sir, from that point that you'll want to know what happened."

"Quite right," said Shelley, "I shall."

"Well, sir," he continued, "she took a taxi on the rank just off Queen's Road. The first one was out of order, so she took the second. I took the third, and ordered the man to follow her. All went well until we got just outside the approach to Paddington Station, and I imagine that it was there that I lost her."

"How do you think that?" asked Shelley.

"Well, sir, there was a bit of a traffic jam, there, owing to several taxis coming out of the station, and I lost sight of the taxi in front for a minute or two. My driver said, though, that he had his eye on the one in front all the time."

"Then why do you think that you lost Miss Latimer there?" asked Shelley.

"Because, sir, we drove on to Trafalgar Square. There the taxi in front stopped, I paid off my man and walked up to the other." Stuart paused impressively. "There was no one in it, sir, and nothing left of Miss Latimer but her hat and coat!"

"She'd hopped out, then, when you were in that jam at Paddington," was Shelley's comment.

"That's the only conclusion I could come to, sir," replied Stuart.

"Where is the hat and coat?" asked Shelley.

"Outside, sir. Shall I get them?" Shelley nodded, and Stuart left the room, to return, carrying a hat and coat which Adolphus recognised instantly as the ones which Margery had been wearing the day before. Shelley examined the clothes minutely.

"Well, Stuart," he said at last, "I suppose it's not your fault. I have another little job for you, before you enjoy your beauty sleep. I know that you've been up all night, but I want you to go along to Miss McKean at the same house as Miss Latimer's, and ask her if Miss Latimer had split her coat. Here, take it along to her if you like. You see, there is a definite split under the arm. Looks as if it might have been someone a little bigger wearing it."

"Do you mean to say, sir," asked Stuart in astonishment, "that it wasn't Miss Latimer who I was following last night?"

"I don't mean to say anything of the sort, Stuart," said Shelley, "I merely notice a somewhat remarkable fact. This coat is a good one, well made and all that sort of thing, but it has parted at the seams under the arms. Both sides, too. I don't think Miss Latimer would willingly have gone out wearing a coat in that condition."

"But I saw her, sir," protested Stuart, "she was quite alone. I saw her face as she passed under the street lamp just along at the end of the road."

"One thing more, Stuart, before you go," added Shelley, "did you see any strange lady go into that house some time—say a quarter of an hour or twenty minutes before Miss Latimer came out?"

"Why do you ask that, sir?"

"Never mind why I ask it," said Shelley impatiently, "answer my question. Probably a lady well wrapped up in furs and so on, so that you couldn't see much of her face."

"As a matter of fact sir, I did see a lady like that. She was wearing a yellow coat and a green hat—horrible colours, both of 'em," answered Stuart, "she went in to the house at about twenty-five minutes after nine. But I don't see. . ."

"Did you see anything at all of her face?" asked Shelley, interrupting his subordinate's loquacity.

"No, sir," said Stuart, ruefully, "she had one of those big floppy hats, well down over her face. And the fur collar of her coat was well pulled up, so that you couldn't see anything at all. I thought that she looked a queer customer."

"She was a queer customer," Shelley told him meaningly, "and if I'm not mistaken, Stuart, my lad, she was the lady whom you followed under the mistaken impression that she was Miss Latimer."

"What evidence, sir?" Stuart was almost speechless at the thought of the cunning way that he had been duped, but he managed to blurt out just those three words.

"Only one little bit of evidence, Stuart," said Shelley, "but I think that it's enough. On the floor of Miss Latimer's room I found a stick of grease-paint. It was, I surmise, taken there by the lady whose trail you struck last night."

"Well, I'll be. . ." Stuart was really speechless by now.

"You can be what you like, Stuart," said Shelley firmly, "but don't be it here. Off with you, now, and see what Miss McKean can tell you about that coat. It will be a bit of extra evidence when we get hold of these gentry. And we'll get hold of them before very long." His face turned grim as he spoke those last words. He was picturing to himself Margery Latimer in the hands of a gang of ruthless criminals. His heart leaped to his throat at the mere thought. He would have to do his best to beat them at their own game. And there was no time to lose.

"What are you going to do now, sir?" asked Adolphus, when Stuart had gone.

"Hullo, you still here?" said Shelley in surprise, "I'd forgotten all about you, Adolphus. You'll have to run home now. I'm afraid that we haven't much chance of finding Miss Latimer for you—at any rate for a day or two."

"You think they've got her?" asked Adolphus.

"Someone has got her, that's certain," said Shelley, "but as to who they are—well, I'm not so certain. Adolphus," he went on, "do you think that Miss Latimer would be the sort to give in to a gang of crooks without putting up a pretty good fight?"

"You bet your life she wouldn't!" said Adolphus.

"That's what I thought," answered Shelley, "and that's why I wonder. . . Well, never mind." He rang the bell on the desk before him, and told the uniformed constable who entered to take Adolphus downstairs, and see that he had a car to take him home.

Even the thrill of going home in a private car did not recompense Adolphus for losing this contact with the great man of Scotland Yard. And the last thing that Adolphus saw, as he turned round to take a final look at the Inspector's room, was Shelley, toying aimlessly with a pencil, gazing before him with a puzzled look in his eyes.

CHAPTER XIX

WHERE IS MARGERY?

SHELLEY was, indeed, very puzzled over the turn of events. He had his suspicions, as has been already indicated, but these did not leave room for an abduction of this kind. This latest development seemed quite impossible to explain.

He sat there at his desk for some time after Adolphus had gone, and then, with a sudden access of energy, he got up, hurried downstairs, and hastened away in his private car.

Along Whitehall, up the Strand and along Chancery Lane he went, stopping outside Mr. Bellingham's office in the last-named thoroughfare.

It seemed, he thought, as if Mr. Bellingham might hold the clue to this sudden change in the tactics of the other side. At any rate, the lawyer knew more about Margery than anyone else, and it was therefore advisable to ask his opinion.

Fortunately, he found the lawyer in his office, a huge pile of unwieldly-looking documents before him, his eyes red and puffed as if with want of sleep.

"Well, Shelley," he snapped, as the detective entered, "what's the trouble now?"

"I'm worried, Mr. Bellingham," answered Shelley, "I thought that I nearly had my hands on the villain at the back of this case, and now something has happened which makes me wonder if I wasn't wrong, after all."

"It seems to me that you fellows are more often wrong than right," answered Bellingham, "and if you are worried, I should think that's your usual state of affairs when a case like this is on. I should be worried if I were in your shoes, I can tell you."

"Miss Latimer has disappeared," announced the detective bluntly, "and isn't that enough reason to be worried?"

For a moment Bellingham looked at him with bewildered eyes. He was quite obviously completely staggered by the news. Then he laughed contemptuously.

"Do you mean to say," he asked, "that you didn't keep a watch on that young lady? Why, she was clearly one of your most important witnesses. Really, Shelley, I'm surprised at you. I begin to think that the stupidities of Scotland Yard, as portrayed in detective stories, must be about right. Miss Latimer vanished, indeed!" And he laughed again, but the detective could not help feeling that there was a certain amount of nervousness hidden behind the laugh.

"She eluded the detective herself," said Shelley, "of course we had someone shadowing her, but she evidently wanted to escape. That was quite clear from the course of events." And, as briefly as he could, he told Bellingham what had happened on the previous night.

"Looks a very pretty little plot, doesn't it?" said the lawyer when he had finished. "Not, mind you, that I agree that Margery was necessarily a free agent in all this. It is quite possible that she was drugged or something, and induced to do this thing."

"You think so?" The detective shrugged his shoulders expressively. "It's the first time that I ever heard of a person who was drugged walking by herself out of a house, and getting away in the way she has—vanishing into thin air, in fact."

"Well, I don't know," said Bellingham, "hypnotism may be the explanation, perhaps."

"Hypnotism is bunk," commented the detective briefly. "That, at any rate, is the conclusion I've come to. I've read a lot about it, but I've never come across a case of it where fraud of some sort doesn't enter in. No, Mr. Bellingham, we have got to make up our minds on the subject. There can be little doubt that she has been enticed away somehow, and that the villain who's at the back of this series of crimes has got hold of her. That, as I said when I came in, is why I'm worried. He's committed four murders already. He won't let a fifth stand in the way, if he thinks that Miss Latimer is likely to be very troublesome to him."

"You think that Cook has got her in his grip?" asked Bellingham briefly.

"I use no names, Mr. Bellingham," said Shelley, "I simply say that I think that the villain of the piece has got Miss Latimer."

"But isn't it obvious?" asked Bellingham. "You know that Margery was positively infatuated with this fellow Cook. She would have it that he was innocent, that he did not have anything to do with the crime, that he had merely run away because he had to have time to clear himself, and all sorts of nonsensical ideas like that."

"I knew all that, Mr. Bellingham," said Shelley soberly, "but I'm not at all sure that they were nonsensical ideas. There's something to be said for psychology, you know, and Miss Latimer had a better idea of the working of John Cook's mind than you or I. He may be innocent, you know. There's an old adage that you should always think a man is innocent until he's proved guilty. That's a useful idea to bear in mind."

"Rubbish!" Mr. Bellingham was very emphatic about it. "I tell you, Shelley, there's not an atom of doubt that he's your man. You will only lose him after all if you try to persuade yourself that there's anything at all in the presumption of his innocence."

"I'm not sure about that, Mr. Bellingham," said Shelley, "and nothing will make me say that a man is guilty of an atrocious crime until his guilt is proved. So you needn't try to persuade me."

"I'm not trying to persuade you of anything," said Mr. Bellingham, "I'm only trying to make you see the facts that are staring you in the face. If this fellow Cook were to write or phone to Margery, telling her to come to him, she would do so without a tremor. In fact, I dare say that's what has happened."

Shelley looked thoughtful for a moment. "I shouldn't be at all surprised if that surmise of yours is right, Mr. Bellingham," he said.

And then he wondered why that look of horror-stricken surprise came over Bellingham's face.

Meanwhile Margery, after having passed a very good night in a very comfortable bed, was making a hearty breakfast. She had not seen John Cook yet, nor had she the remotest idea where she was. The window of the bed-sitting room, plus bath, which was allotted to her, overlooked a wilderness of roofs which might be anywhere in London. There were none of the familiar landmarks to be seen. And her gaoler (for so she thought of him) would answer no questions.

The only human being that she had seen since her arrival at this house of mystery the night before was the young man who had driven her in the taxi—a sure indication, she thought, that he was someone in the employ either of John Cook or of George Washington, Limited. Which was really responsible for her present position she could not make up her mind.

"Can't you tell me why I'm here?" she said to the man, as she enjoyed the beautifully cooked eggs and bacon which he had brought to her, piping hot, for breakfast.

"I'm very sorry, Miss Latimer," he replied, "but my instructions are to tell you nothing at all until my master arrives."

"And who is your master?" she could not help asking.

"That I cannot tell you either," he said, "I can only tell you that you will come to no harm and that this is all done for your own good."

"That's what they used to tell me at school when there was some particularly unpleasant task for me to do," she said, and they laughed together at her little joke.

"Well," he said at length, "there's nothing unpleasant for

you here, unless a day or two of forced confinement in this room, with myself as your gaoler, is unpleasant."

She dropped him a curtsy. "Not at all, kind sir," she said with a smile, and then they laughed again.

"But seriously," she asked him, "can't you give me any idea why I'm here and what's going to happen to me?"

"I can't," he said, "and for a very good reason. That is because I haven't a ghost of a notion myself."

With that he left her, taking the empty plate with him, only to return a few moments later with toast, butter and marmalade.

Margery tried again to persuade him to reveal the secret of the whereabouts of the house, but he was tough as adamant on this question. "I can't tell you." "I don't know, and shouldn't be allowed to tell you if I did." These were the only answers which were vouchsafed her.

Soon he left her alone, with a pile of the latest novels to amuse her, and for awhile Margery tried, vainly enough, to amuse herself with these. But every time that she thought that she was getting really immersed in the book her thoughts persisted in wandering back to the present events. What had been happening to her was so much more exciting than anything that she read in the novels that they seemed pale and feeble in comparison. Why had she been brought here? Where was John? Why had he not been present to receive her on her arrival? Was he in danger? Was she in danger? Were the police on her track yet?

These and countless other questions kept revolving in her mind, like some endless string of vehicles on a merry-go-round, until Margery thought that she would go mad unless she could get an answer to some of them.

No answer was forthcoming, however, and her lunch was served, still by the ex-Oxford taxi driver, in complete silence. She had no desire to speak to him, since he would not or could not answer her questions, and it seemed that he did not particularly hanker after conversation either. So the meal was completed without a word being spoken by either of them.

Then he left her again, and she was immediately immersed in a sea of questions again. More to distract her thoughts than anything else, she studied the landscape which was visible from the window. It was not an attractive vista, but it was something more interesting than sitting down and trying vainly to interest herself in boring novels. Or so she thought, anyhow.

And then she started suddenly. Surely, she thought, there was something vaguely familiar about that building that she could see, rearing its gaunt height above the wilderness of surrounding lower roofs. It was a big building, constructed of some whitish stone, and its roof was flat. It was, in fact, a typically modern building of flats.

It looked, from this distance, very like the new block of flats which had recently been erected in Queen's Road, Bayswater, not more than a hundred yards from her lodging. "Queen's Court," they called the place, and Margery had often admired the building as she passed. A very typical piece of ultra-modern architecture, it was.

But surely this could not be the place? They would never have taken her across London and back again, would they? And then she remembered that there was a noise which she had heard the night before in the taxi. Just before reaching this place she had heard the whistle of a train, and the rattle of shunting coaches. If this were indeed Bayswater that would have been Paddington which they had passed again.

For the first time Margery felt a tremor of fear. Was it just possible, after all, that John Cook was the villain that everyone except herself believed him to be? Could he have kidnapped her with the intention of hiding such evidence as she had to give? She dismissed her fear as absurd. And how, indeed, could he know of that evidence, seeing that she had told no one save only Mr. Bellingham and the Egyptian assistant of George

Washington?

She could not, on further reflection, decide whether or not she had ever told John that she saw him on that dreadful night, now seeming so long ago, when the first murder had taken place, but, in any case, she thought, it did not matter much, seeing that matters were now taken completely out of her hands.

The gaoler arrived at this moment with tea, and left her again immediately, the appetising-looking cakes and the tea-pot on the tray before her.

She did not begin to eat immediately, however. She walked across the room, and looked at that tall white building again. Was it the building in Bayswater which she knew? Or was it merely that she had been deceived by a merely external resemblance between two buildings? After all, she told herself, many of these very modern buildings were very much alike, and it was quite possible that this was somewhere on the northern outskirts of London, as she had at one time supposed.

She found the tea very hot, but, because she was thirsty, she drank it hurriedly, almost burning her tongue in the process.

When she had finished, her gaoler came back.

"Are we in Bayswater?" she asked him suddenly, and she felt sure that he started.

"I can answer no questions, Miss Latimer," he said, but he went across to the window and looked out for a moment.

Margery was sure that she had been right in her surmise. He was trying to see what it was that had put her on the track of this discovery. But he said nothing more, and he left the room, carefully locking the door behind him, as he had done on former occasions.

After he had gone Margery felt unaccountably sleepy. It was strange, for the time was early. It was, indeed, only a little after five o'clock, and yet she had an impulse to lie down on the bed.

For awhile she fought against this desire, but it was

overpowering. So she lay on the bed, and felt herself gently dropping off to sleep. Then, with a great effort of will she recalled herself to her senses. Of course! That was it! The tea had been hot, and it had tasted somewhat strange. She had been drugged! And now, whilst she was asleep, she did not know what would happen.

She got off the bed, and tried to walk across the room. But her legs refused to obey the promptings of her sluggish will. Before she had gone many steps, her weary limbs gave way beneath her, and she pitched on the ground—unconscious! Silently the door opened, and willing hands took her up, and placed her on the bed. Then they were gone and the door was locked once more. Silence reigned supreme.

CHAPTER XX

MARGERY ESCAPES ONCE MORE

As Margery came to her senses, she looked around her curiously, wondering where she could be. This, she thought, was not her bedroom, nor her bed. And she was lying on it fully clothed! And then, suddenly, remembrance came to her. She remembered that she had been brought to this place in the closed taxi, she remembered the day when she had been waited on by that remarkable taxi-driver, and, at last, she remembered the occasion when she had been drugged. ...At any rate, the influence of some drug was the only explanation she could offer for her sleeping like that, in the middle of the day.

She tried to sit up in bed, but the effort sickened her and her head spun around alarmingly. She forced herself to look at her watch. Its hands pointed to the hour of seven. It was broad daylight, and it was thus impossible, on such a bright, summery day, to say whether it was morning or evening. She rather thought that it must be morning, in which case she had slept for more than twelve hours—considerably more, since it was only just after an early tea that she had lapsed into unconsciousness.

Her head was rapidly improving now, and soon she was able to walk, rather shakily, around the room. Nothing seemed to be changed. It was still the rather smartly-furnished bed-sitting-room which it had been before, and even the novels which she had vainly tried to read on the previous day were still there in an untidy pile on the table.

But now Margery was not in the comparatively easy frame of mind which she had been in on that day. She was very definitely alarmed. She had, she remembered, asked her gaoler whether she was in Bayswater, and he had replied that he was not permitted to answer any questions. Or had he replied at all? She could not remember the details, but she did think that this drugging had followed her disclosure of her suspicions.

Was she, then, a prisoner of the enemy? It certainly seemed as if she was. She could not imagine that John Cook would order her to be drugged like this. It was impossible that any reason could be sufficiently urgent for it. Therefore the unknown enemy must have her in his grip.

Instantly she began to formulate plans for escape. The window, of course, was hopeless. The chimney repelled her with disgust, when she looked up it. She could not see herself climbing up its sooty length and getting away via the roof. And in any case it was probably far too narrow to allow the passage of an adult human being.

There remained only the door. And when the door opened there would be certain to be a gaoler there who must be overcome before there was any chance of her escaping.

She glanced round the room hurriedly. He might arrive at any moment now, and it was urgent that she should find some weapon before that time.

On the table there was nothing. He would not be likely to be easily intimidated, this gaoler of hers.

Where, then, could she find something which would serve as a suitable weapon? And then she gasped, with a sudden access of delight. There, on a little shelf which hid an ugly corner of the room, there was a marble statuette. It portrayed a man who was rescuing a damsel from the chains of slavery. Some Greek mythology, Margery told herself, one part of her mind working quite independently of the rest.

Well, this man would rescue another damsel from slavery— or worse. That was the thought which made her chuckle to herself.

Her aching head was definitely on the mend now. There was no doubt that she would be a match for any defenceless man, she thought. And even though she felt some twinges of conscience at the deed which was before her, she knew that it was quite unavoidable. If she was to escape from this room, it was necessary that her gaoler must be, for the moment at any rate, knocked out. And to do that, this was the only weapon available.

Grimly, she seized the statuette. It was marble, all right, and heavy. It would serve her purpose.

What she intended to do if she got out of the room, she dared not think. It was the most desperate of gambles, for there might be countless others outside the room, who would do their level best to prevent her from leaving the house. But she would have to chance that. For the moment, all her faculties were concentrated on getting away from this room. That done, the future would have to look after itself.

Then she stiffened suddenly. She had heard the approach of footsteps on the stairs. She grasped the statuette grimly in her right hand, and waited beside the door, prepared to strike the moment that it opened.

Slowly the footsteps approached, and then halted outside her door. She heard the jingle of keys, as the man fitted one in the lock. The door opened gradually, an inch or two at a time, and the man gazed in. Fortunately, she was standing far enough back for her not to be visible from the doorway, until the man was right in the room. Also, the bed was not fully visible from the doorway either. Only its foot could be seen.

The man came in, and . . . CRASH! Margery brought down the marble statuette on his head with all the force which she could command, and the man dropped, like a log to the floor.

He was, she saw, the chauffeur who had driven the taxi the day before. He was completely knocked out, and Margery felt a little sick as she watched the blood slowly oozing from a wound in his head. It was no time for scruples, however.

She suddenly realised that his fall had made an unearthly crash, which might well rouse anyone else who might happen to be in the house. She pulled him well inside the room, a great effort for her particularly in her present weak state, and then locked him in, removing the key from the door.

The key was on a ring, with a dozen others, and these she thrust into her handbag, which she had somehow remembered to bring with her. Then she turned to go down the stairs. How to get to the street was the next question. And it was, she soon saw, not by any means an easy question to answer.

For as she got to the end of the first flight of stairs, her heart jumped suddenly. Someone was coming up the stairs below! There was no time to turn back, no time to do anything save hide herself where she was—and that as quickly as was possible. In a few moments the newcomer would be upon her.

And then, with a great sigh of relief, she saw the way out. Just before her was an open door. Whether it would provide an effective hiding-place she could not guess. For the moment it was her only possible hiding.

"Bill, where are you?" said a voice outside. Margery thrilled with the knowledge that it was the voice of the Egyptian who had interviewed Mr. Bellingham and herself at George Washington's on that eventful day which now seemed so long ago.

"Bill," shouted the man again, "will you have the kindness to tell me what's the matter?"

In spite of her imminent peril Margery could not help smiling at the incongruity of the polite phrases and the tone in which they were spoken. The Egyptian was very badly scared, it was clear.

"What's all the row about?" asked another voice which she did not recognise.

"Bill went up to see if the girl had come to yet, and he hasn't come down," answered the Egyptian, "I'm worried about him."

"Needn't worry, my boy," answered the other, with a hoarse chuckle, "probably she's fallen for him, and Bill is enjoying a bit of a flirtation, like. He's a good-looker, is our Bill, and he's always liked a bit of fluff."

"That, my friend," said the Egyptian, and his voice was cold and grim, "is nonsense. Bill may like to flirt with the ladies when he is off duty. I know nothing about that and care less. But he knows better than to waste his time when he is on duty here. Besides, didn't the boss tell us that this girl is to be guarded with every atom of care that we've got? Bill wouldn't be fool enough to trespass on the boss's preserves, you know."

"It's my opinion," said the other man, coming up the stairs, and talking in a more conversational tone, "that the boss is goofy over this girl. I reckon it's damned foolish to mix up business and pleasure. But you never can tell. I thought that the boss had enough sense to know that our business, at any rate, won't mix with the romantic stuff. He seems to have fallen all right, though."

"You may be right," said the Egyptian, "but in any case, it does not answer my question. Where is Bill?"

"Upstairs in room twenty-seven," said the other man, "enjoying himself with our fair young prisoner. You forget, my lad, that Bill was a gentleman before he became a——"

"Hush!" The Egyptian interrupted him, and Margery could almost see him holding up an admonitory hand.

"You should be careful, you know," he added, a moment later, "you never know in a place like this. There may be spies in our midst. G. W. would never forgive us if he thought that we'd given away his business."

"That's so," said the other man grudgingly, "and, besides, Scotland Yard may be hanging around, not to mention the other gentry who you and I know something about."

"But what about going up, and seeing what's the trouble?" asked the Egyptian.

"I'm with you there," answered the other man, "you never know when there may be trouble in the air. And we should get the sack from the boss all right if this job went wrong. He's set his heart on winning this trick. And besides, we all know what will happen to him if we make a mess of it."

"The gallows is not a very pleasant place, eh, my friend? That is what I think, anyway," said the Egyptian softly, and they went on up the stairs.

Margery scurried forth from her hiding-place, and went down the stairs as quickly as she could.

Her mind, working with supernatural clearness, was going over the conversation which she had just heard. "The boss," they had said, and "G. W." Obviously George Washington was the leader of a gang of crooks. That seemed to her to be the only possible explanation of the discussion between the two men. Who George Washington might be, she could not imagine. He was clearly someone whom she knew, since the men had referred to him as someone who had "fallen for" her. And, in spite of the fact that she was still in the midst of perils, she could not help wrinkling up her fastidious little nose at the use of that American phrase. No one, at any rate, could use the words "fallen for" when describing the way in which John Cook regarded her. A more old-fashioned phrase must be found to describe that very old-fashioned but still very fashionable emotion.

By now she was on the ground floor, and she proceeded with considerable caution. Probably, in this house of criminals, there would be some sort of door-guard. It was, at any rate, certain that she would not be able to walk out of the door calmly, as one would from an ordinary house.

As she reached the bottom of the stairs, proceeding with the utmost care, so that she should not make a sound to disturb the man who might be there, she saw that she was right.

Inside the front door of the house there was a little recess. In that recess there was a chair. And on the chair there sat a man. He looked just like the ordinary commissionaire whom one sees everywhere nowadays. He wore the uniform of the

Corps of Commissionaires and he was meditatively filling a well-worn briar pipe from a pouch.

All this, Margery felt sure, must be mere camouflage. He was, no doubt, one of the gang, and was placed here in this unassuming guise so as to take in any passer-by who might be surprised to see a man for ever waiting in the doorway of a house. A commissionaire one would expect to see anywhere. And Margery felt compelled to admit that there was a touch of genius in the plan.

But how was she to get past him? That was the great problem. And then she remembered how, in a novel read long ago, the hero had been faced by just such a problem as this. She remembered, too, how he had solved it.

Whether her wits would be quick enough to solve her problem in the same way, she did not know, but it was worth trying. And now every moment became more important. In the back of her mind, she had the picture of the Egyptian and the other man standing outside that door upstairs, wondering why there was no answer to their cries, and then, at last, getting an answer, a groan from the man whom she had knocked out. That his unconsciousness could not last long she knew. And so she had to act and act quickly.

She saw that the commissionaire was busily engaged with his pipe, and she hurried into the room which immediately faced the bottom of the stairs. It was empty. That she could see, for the door was open wide. Once in there she was able to mature her plan.

Open on the table was a book, and this was an object of about the size that she required for her purpose.

Outside the door the passage went back to a door at the rear of the house, a door, she supposed, that led to the kitchen. This door was ajar, and Margery, leaning out of the door of the room, hurled the book, with all her might, at this kitchen door.

Inwardly blessing the fact that she had gone to a school

where the girls played cricket, and so had learned to throw with reasonable accuracy, she heard the book hit the kitchen door with a resounding crash.

She crouched back in the room, holding her breath with the excitement of the moment, and watching intently through the crack of the door.

She heard the hiss as the commissionaire shut the zip-fastener of his tobacco-pouch, and then he got to his feet and hurried along the passage past the room in which Margery was.

Peering out of the room she saw him approach the kitchen door and go out through it, the haste of his steps indicating his sense of the fact that there was something very wrong here.

Quickly and quietly Margery hurried along the passage and out into the street.

At last she was free! She looked around to see the number of the house, and the position which it occupied in the road, and then, with the instinct of a Londoner, she made off in the direction of the main street which could not be, she thought, very far away.

When she reached it she was, although surprised, not particularly so. A large building which seemed somehow familiar hove into sight. It could not be . . . Yes, it was . . . Whiteley's! She was in Queen's Road after all! Her idea that, after all, the closed taxi had taken her for a drive round London, and finally brought her back to her starting-place was right.

Well, she thought, the first thing to do was to take this news to Shelley at Scotland Yard. It was too urgent to be told on the telephone.

At this moment, however, she met an old friend. There, smiling down at her in pleased surprise was Mr. Bellingham.

"This is a surprise, Margery," he said, "wherever have you been? We've been worried sick about you."

"I've just escaped," she told him, "and I'm on my way to Scotland Yard to tell Mr. Shelley all about it. I feel rather faint, though," she added, "and I wonder if we could sit down somewhere."

"Of course," he said, "come along to my flat, my dear. You shall have something to drink, and then you will feel better." He led her along the road a little, and then into a building. It was a tall white building, and there was a lift.

Margery was almost in a dream. She felt, rather than saw, the comfort of the room into which she was taken. She had not known that Mr. Bellingham had a flat in Bayswater, but she was glad, now, to know that he had. Gratefully she settled herself into the chair which he gave to her, and gratefully she drank the refreshing drink which he brought.

"And now, my dear Margery," he said, "you shall tell me all about it."

CHAPTER XXI

MYSTERIOUS MR. BELLINGHAM

"A LL about what?" asked Margery.

Mr. Bellingham's query had rather surprised her. Somehow, she had not thought of this grey-haired man as being particularly interested in the mysteries and puzzles which seemed to have been surrounding her of late.

"All about our dear friend Cook," answered Mr. Bellingham with a kindly smile, "I imagine that you have been staying with him since I saw you last."

"I have been staying," said Margery dramatically, "with the murderer of those four men."

Bellingham laughed aloud. "I'll guarantee that you haven't!" he said.

"Why do you say that?" asked Margery, alarmed in some vague way.

"I'll explain fully later," said Mr. Bellingham, "at the moment, my dear Margery, I think that you owe me a little explanation. After all, Inspector Shelley and I have been worrying our heads off about you, you know. The last few hours have been a very trying time for me."

As Margery looked at him, she thought that it seemed like it. He was an old man: there could be no doubt about it now. His face was grey and wrinkled, and beads of perspiration stood out on his forehead. Inwardly, Margery wondered at that. It was not very hot, and there seemed no sufficient reason for such excitement as would induce them.

But she did not show him the wonder which she felt. She just told him the story of her adventures, as simply and as clearly as she could. He had given her a cigarette, and she puffed away at this between sentences.

When she finished her story she watched the thoughtful expression on his face.

"You did not see Cook at all in this house?" he asked.

"No!" Margery was indignant. The mere suggestion that John Cook might be concerned in an outrage which included the drugging of herself seemed the wildest of impossibilities.

"But he was there, Margery, my dear, he was there," returned Mr. Bellingham, "you may make no mistake about that."

"Why are you so sure?" asked Margery.

"Because, my dear young lady," he returned, "your dear precious friend John Cook is going to hang! He is a murderer and he will shortly pay the penalty of his crimes! You must lead me to the house, Margery, my dear."

"Never!" Margery was really alarmed now. Did this man have some evidence in his possession, evidence which would prove John Cook's guilt? It was impossible, unthinkable. And in any case she was not going to do anything that would help to put a rope around John's neck.

"Why do you answer 'never'? Because you are afraid that your dear lover may be hanged?" Bellingham was openly sneering now, and Margery winced at the bitterness of his tone and the hidden cruelty of his words.

"John Cook is innocent, and you know it!" she replied.

"I may know something about it," answered Bellingham, "and one thing that I know very well is this: the case against your friend John Cook is so black that I doubt if anything at all could save him now, when once the police lay their hands on him."

"In the face of that, do you expect me to lead you to the house where he may be hiding?" asked Margery.

"Strange to say, I do!" returned Bellingham grimly.

"Well, and if I refuse?" asked Margery, trembling. What card had this man hidden up his sleeve? He no longer looked like the kindly guardian whom she had known. There was an evil look in his face, an ugly leer which disfigured that usually kindly countenance.

"If you refuse. . .?" Bellingham looked faintly amused. "If you refuse, my dear Margery, I should not like to say what would happen to you."

"Vague threats will not impress me, Mr. Bellingham," said Margery, "and so I ask you to let me go. No good can come of our carrying on this conversation any further."

"Haughty, haughty!" Mr. Bellingham chuckled. "And that, my dear, is quite right. As a matter of fact, I don't see that we can do much good by talking much more. I shall have, however, to put certain other facts before you."

Margery got up and walked to the door. But he was too quick for her. He dashed ahead of her, turned the key in the lock and rapidly turned around, the key safely in his pocket.

"And," he said, with a smile, "I should not advise you, my dear Margery, to scream or anything of that sort. These flats are supposed to be sound-proof. But, to be just on the safe side, I should be compelled to gag you if you insisted on doing anything more energetic than speaking in the usual conversational tone. You do not mind, I hope, my dear," he added, "if I remove some of these impedimenta." He put his hand up to his head, and Margery gasped! He seemed to be pulling off that grey hair which she had known so long! Then she realised that it was a wig.

"Excuse me," he said, and walked into an ante-room beyond. He emerged a few moments later, and Margery wondered that she had ever taken him to be an old man.

Clean-shaven, wrinkle-less. No grey hair, just a mop of coal-black locks. A young man, and a very energetic one! His very carriage and his walk seemed different.

"Mr. Bellingham!" she gasped.

"Mr. Bellingham no longer, Margery," he said, "but Hardy Coles, Esq., commercial traveller, who has been inhabiting this flat off and on for eighteen months or so. I thought that it might help you to come to your decision if you realised that I have a way out."

"What do you mean?" Margery was really frightened now.

"I mean just this," he said, "if you do not reveal to me the house where I can find John Cook there will be another unsolved murder for Detective-Inspector Shelley tomorrow morning."

"Then you . . . you . . ."

"Oh, yes," he said cheerfully, "I killed those men. But not a soul suspected me. And not a soul is going to now. That's nothing. The point is that I've got to know where John Cook is at this moment. And you're the only person who can tell me. It was a piece of sheer good luck that I met you in the street today. It was risky, of course, coming here in my Bellingham disguise, but somehow I don't think that I shall need to use that much longer."

"How long have you been disguised like that?" asked Margery.

"A good few years," he answered. "You remember, I expect, that there was one period during your school career when you did not see your dear guardian, Mr. Bellingham, for nearly a year. Well, that was when I was making myself word-perfect in the part."

"But . . . but . . . why?" Margery was almost speechless.

"Because, my dear, nothing helps a criminal like having a dual identity. Others have tried it before, but they never did as I have done. They never took on the identity of a real man for their second life."

"Then where is Mr. Bellingham? The real Mr. Bellingham, I mean."

"Oh, him!" The man was openly amused. "He died, you know. A most regrettable accident during his holiday in Switzerland during that year when you did not see him."

"Did you kill him?" Margery was past all horror now.

"Some unkind critics might suggest that I did," said the man, "but I don't think it can be proved. If an oldish man goes mountaineering, accidents are liable to happen, you know."

"But your face . . . the wrinkles . . . you looked an old man."

He laughed again, and it was not a pleasant laugh. "In my unregenerate days," he said, "I was an actor. I knew all the tricks of the trade, and I found another trade in which they would pay better."

"And why do you want to get John Cook?" said Margery, bringing the conversation back to the place from which it had started.

"That, my dear, is too long a story to tell you now," he said, "suffice it to say that he is the only man in the world, I fancy, who has any idea of who I really am. Hardy Coles, I need hardly tell you, is another fiction who will dissolve into thin air as soon as I want him to. Hair cut in a different way, a thick black moustache grown, and Hardy Coles is no more. He's only a temporary sort of person, poor fellow."

"And what do you want me to do?" asked Margery.

"Tell me where John Cook lives," he said. "That is all. You shall have your reward."

"My reward." Margery repeated the phrase thoughtfully. "And what will that be?"

"It will be something which most people are inclined to rate pretty highly," he said, "in other and plainer words, your life!"

"You will kill me otherwise." Margery's heart was thumping against her ribs, and she was amazed that she could speak so calmly.

"I shall kill you otherwise." His voice was still on that even, conversational note. "It is regrettable, I admit. I shall be sorry to do it, but it cannot be helped. You see, my dear Margery, you know too much. You might repeat these things to my dear friend Detective-Inspector Shelley." He paused, and then "What's that?" he said, and hurried into the ante-room.

Soon however he returned, a smile on his face.

"What was the trouble?" asked Margery.

"Thought I heard a noise in there," he said, "but it must have been imagination. My nerves are not what they might be. Difficult to keep a dual rôle going all day long, you know."

"My answer you must know," said Margery, "I cannot give away John Cook. And in any case, my knowledge would be just as dangerous if I did give him away. My—er—elimination would still be necessary." And she tried bravely to smile, in spite of her fears.

"As to that, my dear," he said, and there was something odious in the familiar phrase now that she recalled that this man was probably the murderer of her guardian, "there are two opinions. Personally, I have always erred, I fear, on the side of mercy. I should let you go free. But not in this country. You did not know, I expect, that I have a fast motor-launch down at Gravesend. You would be taken on that, and I could land you somewhere where you would be quite helpless. That is, if I could not persuade you to come in with me on one or two little deals I have ahead."

"You know that that's no use," she said.

"I suppose I do," he said, "as a matter of fact, I could do with a girl like you. It was really with that in view that I took you on in the office. But somehow I always felt that you might have foolish scruples, and I felt that it would be asking for trouble to get you in on any of my schemes of that kind."

"Were you always a criminal?" she asked, "have you no decent impulses whatever?"

He smiled with the utmost good-humour. "Now, my dear Margery," he said, "you are only trying to annoy me. From one who has just been offered her life from a man who has every impulse to murder her, that is distinctly rich."

"Well, in any case, you have had my answer often enough," said Margery, "you know that I would not have betrayed John Cook even when I thought that he was guilty. Now that I know that you are really the murderer, I couldn't think of doing it."

"Pity," he said. "Pity. It would have saved me a few hours' hard work, and it would have saved your life, if you had permitted me to use your aid. However, since it was not to be . . ." Suddenly he grabbed her around the waist, and, before she had time to scream, he clasped his hand firmly over her mouth. Before she knew what was happening she was tightly bound to a chair, her own handkerchief tied over her mouth.

Mutely, she made signs, as well as she could that she wanted the handkerchief removed.

"You will promise not to scream?" he asked, and she nodded. Thereupon he removed it.

"I wanted to ask," she said, "who was the man who tied me up like this, in John's office?" She was sure that if she managed to waste sufficient time, either Shelley or John Cook would save her. Somehow, she must try to keep this man engaged in conversation for as long as possible. Then there might be hope of a rescue. It seemed totally impossible that this should be happening in modern London.

In answer to her question he only smiled at first. Then he spoke. "I hope I do not shock you," he said, "but the gentleman who acted as my emissary then was your dear friend Williamson, now deceased."

"You killed him, too," she asked.

"I killed him, too," he admitted, "and I do not regret the fact. He was a despicable creature and he knew too much about me to be allowed to live. He knew of this place, for example."

"But why all these murders?" said Margery. "It all seems so . . . pointless, you know."

"That, I fear, would be too long a story to be told at present," he said, "it's connected with the National Anti-Speed Association, as I expect you have already guessed."

She nodded.

"The motor-trade," he went on, "is, as you may know, in queer street at the present time. All these new import duties, changing taxation on cars and the streamline idea. They've all come together, more or less. And when a new invention altogether comes along, an invention which looks like revolutionising motor-transport, there are always people who will pay for advance information. That's how I stumbled on the thing. I can tell you no more, and, I expect, do not need to. But your vivid imagination will enable you to fill in the details."

He turned his back on her again, and when he came around to her side of the room once more she could hardly suppress the scream that rose, unbidden, to her throat.

"Pretty little toy, isn't it?" he said, playing with the knife in his hand. "Extraordinary thing, I always think that people want to play with nasty, noisy things like pistols and revolvers. A knife is so much safer and so much quieter. I always use one, anyhow." And he tested the point on his hand.

"But the blood!" said Margery, "doesn't it alarm you?"

"My dear Margery," he said pleasantly enough, "you surely don't think a man who has successfully managed all those murders is scared of a little blood?" There was a wild look in his eyes, and Margery realised, what she had been suspecting for the past ten minutes or so, that this man was, in every sense of the word, a madman.

"Oh, no," he said, reading her thoughts with almost uncanny precision, "I'm not mad. For instance, I had the bathroom of this flat lined from floor to ceiling with tiles, with just such an occasion as the present one in view. Blood washes off tiles easily, you know."

"And now," he went on, after a momentary pause, whilst he tested the point of the knife against his hand, "I think that the moment, my dear Margery, has come." He seemed to have forgotten all about Cook. His only desire seemed to be to kill. Margery remembered reading a book by some learned criminologist in which the writer had suggested that a murderer found pleasure in the actual act of killing. She had thought it a horrible theory at the time, but now she began to understand it.

Her handkerchief was bound over her mouth again, this time with another one rolled into a ball, and thrust inside her mouth, so that it was a perfect gag. He then lifted the chair to which she was bound, lifted it bodily, as if it were of no weight at all, and carried her into the bathroom beyond. He set down the chair just inside the door, and then turned around to her.

"Believe me, my dear Margery," he said, "I am very sorry to do this, but it is, as I have explained to you, quite unavoidable."

"Hands up, Silvester! Drop that knife!" said a voice behind them, and the man who had been known as Bellingham turned around in a panic. Then he dropped the knife hurriedly, and gasped with shocked surprise.

For there, facing him in the doorway of the tiled bathroom, was John Cook!

CHAPTER XXII

ENTER SHELLEY AGAIN

FOR a few moments they stood there, like a group carved in stone. Cook held his revolver steadily in his right hand, its barrel pointing unwaveringly at the criminal. The other man, crouching there, looked at the newcomer with the expression of a snarling beast. He was beaten, and he knew it.

"The game's up, Silvester, and you know it!" said Cook, sternly, and Margery gasped. Silvester? Who was he?

But her questions were not destined to be answered for a moment, at any rate.

"Go over there, Silvester," said Cook, "and untie Miss Latimer. Then step back against the wall. Look slippy, now, or my finger on this trigger might slip too soon. They would bring in justifiable homicide, you know, especially as you have that knife."

Without a word the other man walked obediently towards Margery and untied the ropes which bound her to the chair. Hurriedly she pulled the hateful gag from her mouth.

"All right, Margery?" asked Cook briefly.

"Quite all right, thanks," she answered gratefully, "although I don't quite know what would have happened if you'd been a little bit later."

"I do," he said, "and I know that in that case my finger on this trigger would have slipped." And he glared at the other man with a stony glare.

"But who is this man?" she asked.

"Silvester?" Cook laughed. "I think that Scotland Yard will be able to give you a better answer to that question than I can," he said. "Confidence man, forger, thief, murderer, and Lord knows what else. That right, Silvester?"

"I'm saying nothing," Silvester grunted.

"And very wise, too," said Cook, "but you seem to have forgotten, my lad, that when you told Miss Latimer all about your wonderful doings, I was behind the door. When you heard a sound in the ante-room, that was me. I managed to slip into the bathroom when you looked around, though, and when you carried Miss Latimer through, I was hiding under the table. Very simple, when you know how, isn't it?"

"But what put you on to this stunt?" Silvester permitted himself the one question.

"That's too long a tale to tell you now," said Cook with a smile, "although I daresay that you'll hear it at the Old Bailey before very long. When you're in the dock and I'm in the witness-box, I mean."

Silvester glared at John menacingly, but he could do nothing. His knife was in John Cook's possession, and he had never carried a revolver. As he had said to Margery some time before, he never used a revolver. They were too noisy.

"What's to be done, then?" he asked sullenly, "we can't stay here all evening, looking like the figures in a cheap melodrama. Am I to be allowed to put my hands down, anyhow?" There was, indeed, something rather melodramatic about their position, John Cook with his revolver still pointing straight for Silvester's heart, and the arch-criminal against the wall, his eyes glaring with rage, like those of a hungry beast.

"You are not to bring your hands down, my friend," said John, "and you are not to move from the spot where you stand. I am taking no risks in this business. And anyhow you won't have to endure this for long. Our old friend Shelley will be here soon."

"Shelley?" The man was obviously taken aback at the news.

"Yes," said John, enjoying the other's discomfiture, "Shelley. I phoned the Yard and sent them a mysterious message just before I climbed up the fire-escape outside, and so reached your bathroom. You made two mistakes in choosing this place, Silvester."

"And what were they?"

"First: you should have taken a flat which hadn't got a possible back entrance via a fire-escape. And, second: you shouldn't have chosen a place where there was a very convenient telephone booth just opposite the front door."

"You followed us here?" It was Margery who asked the question.

"Yes, my dear," said Cook. "When you eluded, by a very clever wheeze, my friend Hopkins, the commissionaire, I happened, most fortunately, to be walking along the street outside. I saw you come out into the street, and I knew that something must have gone wrong. I just stopped for a word with Hopkins, and then I followed you. When I saw you speak to friend Silvester here, I knew that the end was very near, so I phoned Shelley at once."

At this moment came a thunderous knock at the door.

"See who that is, Margery, there's a good girl," said John. "Unfortunately, I have to stay with this swine." The bitter enmity in his tone made Margery look up in surprise. But when she remembered the fate that this man had destined for her, she could appreciate John Cook's annoyance.

"Miss Latimer!" It was Shelley who greeted her at the door. "Who'd have thought of seeing you here?"

"Come in, Inspector," she said with a smile. "We have a prisoner for you here."

In surprise, Shelley entered, to chuckle to himself as he saw the tableau which was spread out for his attention.

"Very pretty, very pretty, Mr. Cook," he said, "but is this supposed to be real life, or is it a scene from a play by Edgar Wallace?"

"It's real life, all right," said John, "and it would have been another real death if I hadn't happened to be keeping an eye on Miss Latimer here."

"Who's the prisoner?" asked Shelley.

"Silvester," said John shortly, and Shelley whistled softly to himself.

"Silvester, by all that's wonderful!" he said. "How long ago was it that I arrested you for the Duchess of Julian's pearls, Silvester?"

"Fifteen years," answered that worthy, with some pride in his voice. "Twelve years ago I escaped from Horfield Prison, Bristol, and you fellows have never set eyes on me since—not to know me, that is."

"We knew that you were at work, though," said Shelley, "got your finger-print—right fore-finger—on the door of Henshaw's car. I knew that you were in this murder plot, all right, and suspected that you were the moving spirit of it. But what Mr. Cook here had to do with it, I can't tell at all."

"That's a story that will keep, Shelley," said Cook, smilingly, "but in the meantime, don't you think that it's time that you carried out your arrest? Conversation is all very well in its way, you know, but business before pleasure has always been my motto."

"And very nice, too," said Shelley. And then the pleasant look disappeared from his face, and he strode up to Silvester, and laid his hand on his shoulder.

"James Silvester, I arrest you for the wilful murder of Henry Henshaw, and I warn you that anything that you may say will be taken down . . ."

"I'm saying nothing," said Silvester for the second time, and then, with a sudden twist of his muscular shoulder, he had evaded the detective's grasp.

Margery screamed. She had seen the look of sudden madness which had lit up the criminal's eyes. He dodged John Cook, who tried to grasp him as he ran past, and then, there was a crash of broken glass, a dull thud, and . . . silence, broken only by the roar of London's traffic.

"Better see, I suppose," said Shelley, running into the sitting-room. He looked out of the window, and then rejoined them in silence.

"Well?" said John.

"I suppose it's just as good," said Shelley, "but they do hate this sort of thing at Scotland Yard. Doesn't seem right, somehow, for the criminal to evade trial and all the rest, like this."

"Then he's dead," said Margery.

"This room, Miss Latimer," said Shelley, "is on the seventh story. That yard down below is paved with hard slate slabs. I saw that my Sergeant was picking him up, but it's no go, I'm afraid. I posted a man at each door, as you suggested, Mr. Cook," he added, "and one of them was just outside the window. Must have given him a rare shock, too, when Silvester came hurtling down at him."

"Oh, don't!" It was Margery who spoke, her hands before her eyes.

"I know that it seems like a cruel bad death, Miss Latimer," said Shelley, "but don't you forget those men that he sent to their death."

"I don't forget, Mr. Shelley," said Margery, raising her head, "and I don't forget, either, that if it hadn't been for you and for Mr. Cook, I should have been one of them."

"That's the way to look at it," said Shelley.

"But look here," said Margery, a thought suddenly striking her, "didn't you suspect Mr. Cook of being concerned in these crimes?"

"At one time I did," admitted Shelley, "but not for very long. Not really suspect him, you might say, after Silvester's fingerprint was identified. It was a rare trouble to identify that finger-print, because it was a very poor impression. But then, when we had got that, I felt pretty sure that Silvester was our man. I didn't quite know what disguise he would be using, but I did know that he must be disguised somehow, because he was an old acquaintance of mine. I was only a Sergeant when I arrested him for that pearl robbery, and I remembered him well. It was an interesting case, that, the first really big thing that I was concerned in . . ."

"But, Mr. Shelley," said Margery, trying to stop the flow of reminiscence, "if you didn't suspect Mr. Cook, why did you persist in trying to find out, from me, where he was hidden?"

"Because," said Shelley, cheerfully, "I was quite sure that Mr. Cook knew more about this blooming case than I did. And that's proved true, anyhow." He seemed to find some consolation in the reflection.

"So all that you really wanted to do was to pick his brains?" Margery's question seemed to strike the other two as amusing.

"Well, Miss Latimer," said Shelley, when their laughter had subsided, "that is so. You see, I wanted to get the man who had committed those murders and I knew that he was a very clever man. I also knew that it would have to be a very clever man to catch him. That was pretty obvious, really. And as Mr. Cook was the cleverest man in this case, he was the fellow I had to go after. That was all."

"How did you know that Mr. Cook was the cleverest man in this case?" Margery was insistent, and the two men smiled once more.

"That, my dear, is a tribute to my intellectual face," said John.

"Not altogether that, either," said Shelley, "although I admit, of course, sir, that anyone who looked at your face would know that you were someone a bit out of the ordinary, like."

"Thank you, Inspector. You are very kind," said John, and bowed deeply to the Scotland Yard man, a broad grin creasing his countenance.

"Ah, yes, sir," said Shelley, "but you must know that when I knew who you were your reputation was enough for me. I felt quite sure that you would be able to lay your hands on the criminal, if ever anyone could."

"When he knew who you were?" Margery looked at John in amazement. "Then who are you?"

"John Cook, at your service, dear lady," he said, and bowed to her in her turn.

"Oh, do help me, Mr. Shelley," she said, turning round and looking at the detective appealingly, "you know who he is, and you must tell me what you know."

"Is the lady to know your guilty secret, sir?" he asked, "shall I tell her? Or do you prefer to do the dirty work yourself?"

"I'll do it," said Cook, "as a matter of fact, though, John Cook does happen to be my real name, the name which was given to me by my godfather and godmother in baptism, as they say." He grinned at Margery almost impishly.

"Oh, do tell me!" she said, "if you keep putting me off in this childish way I shall really begin to think that there is something mysterious behind you."

"There are many mysteries behind me," he said solemnly, "and many more inside my head. There: doesn't that tell you anything?"

"It tells me that you are a very foolish young man," she said, "and a young man who wants spanking. Now, who are you? Why all this fuss and bother?"

"Shall I tell her, Inspector?" he asked.

"I should, sir," said Shelley, a twinkle in his eyes.

"Well then, Margery, my dear," said John, throwing out his chest, and slapping himself resoundingly, *à la Tarzan,* "I am the great detective! I am George Washington!"

CHAPTER XXIII

GEORGE WASHINGTON EXPLAINS

THERE was a very select company at John Cook's Hampstead house that night. It consisted of John Cook himself, Detective-Inspector Henry Shelley, Margery Latimer and Sergeant Cunningham. Shelley had thought that, since Cunningham had been in this case almost from the start, he deserved to know what was known of the inner workings of the business. And John had raised no objection to the Sergeant's presence.

They had a pleasant dinner and much frivolous conversation. Shelley chaffed Margery and John unmercifully: it was, he thought, fairly obvious, from the glances which they continually kept casting at each other, that a marriage was in the air. Still, up to the end of dinner, nothing definite was said about the matter. And when the meal was finished, Shelley wished to talk of other things.

"Now, Mr. Cook," he said, "or Mr. Washington, whichever name you prefer . . ."

"Cook," answered the other with a cheery smile, "George Washington is only my *nom-de-plume*, so to speak. And now, I suppose that all the secrecy with which I tried to preserve my anonymity will go west. Such is fame!"

"Afraid it is, Mr. Cook," said Shelley, "we shall have to make most of this affair public, you know. After all, there have been no fewer than four murders in connection with this business, and if we don't make some sort of explanation to the public, we shall have the pressmen growling at our heels for evermore."

"Well, I suppose that I shall have to put up with some publicity in connection with it," said John, "and what is it that you want to know?"

"I want to know all about it," said Shelley, "and I want to know what it's all about. After all, Mr. Cook, I've taken your

197

word that Silvester was the real villain of the piece, and now I want to hear what you've found out about him."

"Right-ho!" said John, "and just stop me if I don't make myself clear. I don't know quite all of the details myself, but I think that I can straighten things out for you pretty well. The whole yarn goes back some eighteen months or so. I don't know, by the way, Shelley, if you know anything at all about the various experiments which are being done in the effort to produce petrol from coal?"

"If it's helpful to you, Mr. Cook," admitted Shelley, "I know quite a lot about it. But I'm afraid that I don't see what that's got to do with this present business."

"As a matter of fact," said John, "it is this present business. You see, about eighteen months ago Mr. Victor Dunn was in a panic. His business was rapidly going downhill, and he didn't for the life of him see how to get it up again. And then, quite suddenly, the thing fell into his lap. A young scientist, whose name doesn't matter in the least, came along to him with a perfect method for getting petrol from coal-tar. He offered the secret to Dunn for a large sum of money, and Dunn managed to get a pretty big combine of the largest motor manufacturers to buy the thing, to be used between them. The reason why they were the people to handle the business and not the oil and petrol firms was that it was necessary for this petrol, which had a very different combustibility from the ordinary stuff, to be used in a specially designed engine."

Shelley nodded. "Something like the heavy-oil engines that they're using in the new London buses," he said.

"That's the idea," John agreed, "and, to cut a long story short, this combine was formed secretly."

"It included, I suppose, the Locke-Macdonald Company," remarked Shelley, with a twinkle in his eye.

"So you knew something about it, eh, Inspector?" said John. "Well, that was where I came in."

"Yes?" Shelley was all attention.

"It came to the ears of the members of this new combine that some rivals had heard of the scheme, and were, so to speak, moving heaven and earth to get hold of the secret. There were several queer things that happened about then, burglaries when nothing was stolen, and so on. They rather got the wind up about it, and so they decided to call in George Washington."

"How did they know that you were George Washington?" This was Margery's question.

"They didn't, my dear," said John, "and they had no idea that the National Anti-Speed Association, Limited, was anything at all to do with them. That was entirely my own idea. As a matter of fact, I made myself absolutely live the part. I talked so much against speed that I almost believed the arguments myself by the end of the job."

"You seemed to me to be very much in earnest about it," said Margery, "so much so that I was almost converted against my will."

John laughed. "That, of course, was the impression I had to give," he said, "it gave me a beautiful excuse for probing into the whys and wherefores of the motor-trade, you see, in my efforts to get on the track of the gentry who were running this show. I had a very pretty little argument, too, if any further excuse was needed, about the motor manufacturers being closely linked up with the manufacture of war material."

"And who were these people who employed you, Mr. Cook?" asked Sergeant Cunningham. It was his first contribution to the conversation.

"Even in the confidence of this room, Sergeant, I'm afraid I can't give you all their names," said John, "but it is, perhaps, enough if I say that three of the directors of the new combine were to be Sir Henry Henshaw, Lord Chaney, and Mr. Victor Dunn."

Shelley whistled. The whole hideous plot was beginning to become obvious to him.

"Did Silvester work for some rival firms?" he asked.

"I'm not quite sure," said John, "I think, as a matter of fact, that he was approached by some unscrupulous business man about the matter, but as soon as he saw that he was on to something really big, he played for himself. He was not a man who would have any hesitation in double-crossing those who employed him, you know."

"Did he commit all the murders himself?" This was Shelley's next question.

"That, I'm afraid we shall never know," said John. "He certainly killed Henshaw. I saw him, myself, when I walked down the street that night. I don't know how he persuaded Henshaw to stop. But, after the murder, I came along, and I hopped into the car quickly, made sure that Henshaw was dead, and got out again. That, I believe, was when Margery first saw me." He smiled at Margery, and she smiled back, that dazzling smile of hers which seemed to intoxicate him. With an effort, however, he recalled himself to his present task, and resumed his story.

"He killed Chaney, of course, just outside his own office. If I'd been a few minutes later I should have caught him red-handed. I believe that he killed Dunn at Slough, but I don't know for sure. It may be that Williamson did the job that time."

Shelley suddenly slapped his knee." Of course!" he cried, "I knew that I'd been overlooking something. It's been worrying me all the evening."

"What has?" asked John.

"Why, just after Dunn was murdered, Silvester, who of course, I only knew as Bellingham then, told me that he had been at Slough with Dunn. He said that he left Dunn shortly before the murder and Williamson corroborated him."

"Of course, Williamson would bear out whatever Silvester had said," John remarked, "you see, Williamson was merely a tool of his. And when Williamson began to go back to his real game, which was blackmail, he killed Williamson."

"But I still don't quite see why, Mr. Cook," objected Shelley, "I see why he had to kill Williamson, of course, but why all the other murders? Why not concentrate on stealing the formula or whatever this secret process was?"

"The details of the process," said John, "were in the vaults of the Chancery Lane Safe Deposit Company. It's rather funny, when you think of it, that the secret for which all these murders were committed was lying there, within a hundred yards or less of the spot where Silvester had his office. But you see it was quite hopeless for him to expect to get the thing out. The only way was to get hold of the key and the documents which one has to produce in order to get into a place like that. And he didn't know which one of the men had it! Now do you see?"

"Do you mean to say that he was prepared to kill all the men concerned, if necessary, in order to get hold of that key?" Shelley was frankly incredulous, whilst Margery was horrified at the thought that this man had been her guardian and employer.

"That is exactly what I do mean to say!" answered John in his most even tones.

"Was he sane?" asked Shelley.

"Well, frankly, I don't think he was," admitted John, "although, mind you, he carried out the most elaborate plans most skilfully. And he was a genius of an actor. You remember those burglaries at my house and at the office. Although Williamson actually did the work, Silvester planned them."

"It was Williamson who answered me when I phoned and asked if you were home?" said Margery.

"Yes," said John, "you see, I puzzled them. They didn't know who I was. And so they had to burgle my places to find what I knew. All my notes were in code, as a matter of fact, so they didn't get hold of much. The fact that they decoyed Margery out to South Kensington that time, and that I called to see her when she was out was a mere coincidence. And they had to burgle the office twice, because the first time they hadn't thought of the fact that things might be under the floor."

"I begin to see," said Shelley slowly, "but why all the elaborate business of tying up Miss Latimer, and then untying her again?"

Margery and John looked at each other solemnly for a moment. Then the humour of the situation became too much for them, and they collapsed, for a few minutes, in helpless laughter.

"I forgot that you didn't know about that, Shelley," he said, "it was I who released Miss Latimer. She was tied up by Williamson. You found, I suppose, that it was Williamson who did all the burglaries?"

"Oh, we found that all right," said Shelley, "you were the person who puzzled us all through."

"I flatter myself," said John, "that the Anti-Speed Association was really a great wheeze. There was only one thing that worried me. I was afraid that you might find out a fact from my guilty past."

"The fact that Mr. John B. Cook won the hundred miles race at Brooklands last year?" said Shelley, with a smile, "oh, we're not quite such ninnies at Scotland Yard as you young people are inclined to think."

For a moment John was quite flabbergasted.

Then he laughed again. "So you knew all the time," he said.

"We knew," said Shelley, "and what puzzled us was that you should be keen enough to do that, and then turn around and work against all that Brooklands stands for."

"Well you know now, don't you?" said John, and Shelley agreed.

"And now," said Margery, "it's my turn to ask questions." They looked at her with surprise.

"Why," said Shelley, "I thought that Mr. Cook had cleared up everything beautifully."

"There are one or two points," said Margery. "First of all,

what was the meaning of a long list of telephone numbers that I found in the office? I rang them up, and asked for you, but they wouldn't tell me who they were, and they none of them knew you."

"Oh, that!" John looked somewhat relieved, she thought. "Those numbers were the branches, in various parts of London, of George Washington, Limited. You see, it's always handy to be able to get hold of someone who shall be able to take on a job at a minute's notice, in any part of town."

"And who were the awful men whom I overheard after I'd escaped from the room in Bayswater?" she went on.

"Awful men! Margery, I'm surprised at you," he said, "they were some of my most trusted assistants, put on the most important job of the lot—guarding you."

"Why was I shut up there?"

"Well, my dear," said John, "I knew that Silvester was getting desperate, and I knew that he would try to strike at me through you. It was absolutely essential that you should be got out of the way for a day or two."

"And was I drugged?" she asked.

"You were," said John, "quite a harmless drug, I assure you, my dear. You see, when Henderson, the man who brought you your food, reported to me that you were getting restive, I thought that it was time that you were quieted down for a bit. And I was justified, for when you got out, you nearly spoiled the whole business by running into Silvester's arms."

"Yes, I suppose that was all right," she said.

"Good," he replied, "and am I forgiven?" Margery gave grudging assent, and then she suddenly remembered another question.

"Why," she asked, "did you allow the Egyptian to give me such awful scares about you, suggesting, when I was there with Mr. Bell—I mean Silvester—that you were in deadly peril?"

"That was to put Silvester off the track," said John, "you see, we couldn't let him know that I was George Washington. And Nawar put that note in your handbag, so you weren't kept on tenterhooks for long."

Soon Shelley and Cunningham found that it was time to go, and John and Margery were left alone.

"And now," said John, "it's my turn to ask questions." But he only had one question to ask, although that was a very important one. And he knew what the answer would be, before he asked it.

"I must ring up Scotland Yard a moment," he said, some time later, "just a moment, dear." Margery was surprised, and stood by his side, whilst he dialled the number.

"Shelley?" he said, after a moment, "I want to know if you'll be free on Monday. Yes? Good. Then please remember that you have an important engagement then. What is it? Oh, nothing very much, really. Just that Margery and I agree that you should be best man. Good night." And he banged down the receiver, a satisfied smile on his face.

THE END

Other Golden Age Detective books published by Galileo (for full listings please go to https://galileopublishing. co.uk/category/golden-age-detective-fiction/).

Curiosity Killed the Cat   Joan Cockin   9781915530141 | £10.99

Villainy at Vespers   Joan Cockin   9781912916900 | £10.99

Dancing with Death   Joan Coggin   9781912916603 | £9.99

Who Killed the Curate?   Joan Coggin   9781915530134 | £10.99

The King and the Corpse   Max Murray   9781915530158 | £10.99

A Bullet for Rhino   Clifford Witting   9781915530271 £10.99

Catt Out of the Bag   Clifford Witting   9781912916375 | £8.99

Dead on Time   Clifford Witting   9781912916634 | £9.99

Let X be the Murderer   Clifford Witting 9781915530004 | £10.99

Measure for Murder   Clifford Witting 9781912916528 | £8.99

Midsummer Murder   Clifford Witting   9781912916733 | £9.99

Murder in Blue   Clifford Witting   9781912916504 | £8.99

Subject Murder   Clifford Witting   9781912916993 | £10.99

The Case of the Michaelmas Goose Clifford Witting

9781915530127 | £10.99